WILY AND THE CANINE PANDEMIC

by Michelle Weidenbenner

Cover Illustrated by Christine Kornacki

R. Publishing, LLC

Published by R. Publishing, LLC.

Text copyright 2017 by Michelle Weidenbenner

Editing by Vie Herlocker

Cover illustration copyright 2017 by Christine Kornacki Illustrations

Cover jacket prepared by Cathy Helms of www.avalongraphics.org

Formatting by Polgarus Studio

Inquiries about this book should be addressed to:
Michelle Weidenbenner
Michelle@MichelleWeidenbenner.com

ISBN: 978-0-9863362-6-3 e-book
ISBN: 978-0-9863362-7-0 paperback

KID REVIEWS

"*Wily and the Canine Pandemic* was amazing. I really enjoyed the story and the characters. I also enjoyed the space ships and Centaurs—wish they were all real. I can't wait to read the next book in this series!" (Matt L., 10 years old)

"A perfectly-paced adventure book I could picture myself in." (Liam C., 10 years old)

"Hypnotic. From the first page about Thor being like a detective, I couldn't put the book down. It was thrilling." (Bryson S., 9 years old)

"Michelle Weidenbenner shows readers the importance of innovation and perseverance in *Wily and the Canine Pandemic*. This book includes lessons on perseverance, courage, assertiveness, and passion to fight for what you believe in and for those you love." (Elizabeth S., 14 years old)

THE SPELL

Chervil, fennel, savory and thyme,
Help to make my words all rhyme.
Bring their meaning to this life,
Cast out Orbita's wanton strife.

Starlight shining sharp and bright,
Give me what is true and right.
The Chiron's love is all I need,
To rule and lead the Centaur steed.

On Orbita, I cast this curse:
Keep her heart to him adverse.
(Turn his heart to only me,
Together for all eternity.)

Stop her selfish monologue.
Turn her into newt or frog.
Replace her beauty, oh, so sweet,
With spotted skin and four webbed feet.

Through lust and toil and briny tears,
Bind this curse two hundred years.
At that time, restore the bride
From princess frog to Centauride

CHAPTER ONE

Thin gray clouds draped across the late morning sky. The warm May sun had fully ascended from the east. Thor lingered in the shadows at Maple Avenue and Center Street in the Indiana suburb of Bluebird, his backside up against the brick building, his heart hammering in his canine chest. He'd spotted the white delivery truck—the one he'd been looking for. It was parked at the curb. After two days, he was finally going to get the chance to get into the truck and see where the driver was taking the dead dogs.

If the driver suspected Thor's identity, things could get complicated in a hurry, so he pretended to sniff the ground, nonchalantly, like other Great Danes, even though he was nothing like other dogs.

The truck driver jumped down from the front seat and skipped to his back door, whistling the tune B-I-N-G-O. He unhitched the bolt and rolled the door up. The wheels clattered.

What a monster, Thor thought. *Doesn't he have any compassion? How can he be happy at a time like this?*

A man called from the porch of a nearby home. "Hey, we need your help." The man cleared his throat as if straining with emotion. "Our boy … was a mastiff."

The driver went to collect the dog.

This was Thor's chance. He padded to the truck's rear door and leaped up, throwing himself on top of a mound of dead dogs. The stench gagged him. *Talk about body odor.*

Seconds later, the driver's footsteps grew close. He huffed and grunted. "This … has got to be … the heaviest load … of … the day," he said under his breath.

The truck bed shifted with a thud.

Thor pictured the dead mastiff being chucked beside him. A fly buzzed in his ear. He didn't dare shoo it away. He played dead. He couldn't risk getting caught—especially now. He kept his eyes closed and stayed limp, his tongue hanging out of the side of his mouth.

When the door jangled shut, Thor risked opening his eyes. The mastiff lay next to him, his eyes bulging.

Sorry, guy. I bet your family is grieving. Thor moved his paw across the mastiff's eyes to close them. The truck lurched forward. Thor covered his nose with both of his paws.

Let's hope this doesn't take long.

If Thor had planned right, the driver would stop soon. That would give him and Mindia the chance they needed. Mindia was floating in the invisible space shuttle nearby, following them, ready to help him out. Something smelled like cat pee in Thor's territory, and he didn't like it. He would get to the bottom of what was happening and bring the info back to his team.

He hoped he wouldn't have to ride in the flea-infested heap much longer. It would take him forever to get rid of those biting insects.

The truck slowed, then jerked into park. Thor waited in his dead position. The driver's door opened and closed and his humming grew louder. Distant whistling trickled in through the door, drawing closer.

Mindia, where are you? Hurry with the distraction.

Thor shut his eyes just as the door rolled open. An awful stench scorched his nostrils—worse than the smell in the pit with the dead dogs. This reeked of singed hair and burning dog flesh.

"I need a cart," the driver said to himself.

"Excuse me," Mindia's sweet voice finally sounded. "Could you tell me where 101 Parker Street is?"

Thor exhaled. *Thank goodness. Not a moment too soon.*

"Sure, it's ..." the driver said. His voice grew more distant, like he was moving toward Mindia.

Thor fluttered one eye open, then stood on all fours and peeked out of the truck. The driver was facing Mindia. The dog leaped out of the truck, hid behind a trashcan, and watched Mindia spiral her eyes at the man, taking possession of his mind.

The driver's jaw went slack as the hypnosis overtook him.

Well done, dear girl. Thor approached the building as planned. Aha. It was the abandoned Justin Mill Factory.

Mindia waved for him to go inside.

He padded behind the driver and tiptoed through a door and into the old factory. The hallway was dark, but he could hear distant voices and the whirring of machines.

He followed the sound until he got close to the voices, then peered through a hole in the wall. Dead dogs were placed on conveyer belts and workers in brown scrubs and blue facemasks and hairnets leaned over each dog. Each worker held a syringe with a three-inch needle. They pierced a dead dog at the spine and extracted fluid. Then they filled glass vials with the liquid.

Huh? Thor ducked when a worker turned toward him. His heart pounded. Had she seen him? He waited.

No. She must not have because nothing happened. He stole another glance.

Once the fluid was extracted, the dogs continued down the conveyer line until they ended at an incinerator where they fell into the large metal canister and burned to ashes. Each body stiffly plopped on top of the other, their love and companionship a thing of the past.

A lump formed in Thor's throat. So many people would be sick to see this. At least now he understood a part of the puzzle. Whoever was behind this was taking something from a dead dog's spine. But what and why?

Above the factory area was a balcony. A navy-suited man smirked from the top, watching the workers below. He sounded an air horn and said, "Break time. Be back in fifteen minutes. That's all."

Instantly, the conveyer belts halted. The workers left their posts and headed toward a room in the back, talking to each other on their way, like robots obeying a command. But they weren't robots. They were people, people who were probably getting paid by some evil person.

When the suited man retreated to a room behind him, and the workers were out of sight, Thor continued past the hole in the wall and down the hallway to the large production area where the workers had been. He tiptoed on all fours past rows of dead dogs. The stench reminded him that he was only a few steps away from being incinerated. He bounded up the stairs toward the offices, trying to avoid his toenails tapping on the concrete treads. He needed to get as close as possible to the creeps so he could identify them—the ones who'd started this whole mess.

The truck driver entered the factory below, whistling.

Thor ducked behind a dumpster and watched the driver who scanned the room, spotted a grocery cart, reached for it, and headed back outside.

Mindia could only detain him for so long. After a few minutes, her control wore off. He'd have to thank her later. Such a sweet girl. It was too bad about her situation. She really wanted to get home, but the Dark Horse would have no part of it. She was far too valuable.

Thor ducked out of sight and squinted, waiting for the driver to return with the cart of dead dogs. He'd be back. Thor would have to pay attention. Meanwhile, he crouched low at the top of the stairs, beneath the office window.

The punk inside the office was on the phone. "We've taken in a record amount. About 2,480 today. Good day. If this keeps up, we'll be at 1.5 million by the end of the month." He paused. "No, there's no way I'm reporting them. They've stolen so much from me. I don't owe them a penny. I don't feel bad about taking their money." He laughed, and a few minutes later he hung up.

Thor needed to get into the office to obtain the evidence.

A door opened below and heavy footsteps sounded on the concrete steps. Someone, maybe more than one person, climbed the stairs.

Thor scooted around the corner and hid behind another garbage can. He didn't dare look.

The footsteps drew closer and the guy who had been on the phone demanded, "Hey, what are you doing—"

But the goon's words were cut off by two quick muffled sounds. *Had he been shot?*

Thor's heartbeat raced. He peeked around the corner and sniffed. The fragrance of expensive cologne hung in the air. Two men in blue suits dragged the other guy out by the arms, his body limp, his head bobbing onto his chest, his feet scuffing the floor … was he dead?

Thor gulped. He wished he could see the faces of the men, but all he saw were their backs.

As they shuffled down the stairs, one of the killers shouted to the workers who had returned to their stations, "Get back to work, and don't make any trouble."

The factory's conveyer belt started again, the machine's whirring sound dominating the air.

Now's my chance, Thor thought. His mouth was as dry as a cat's tail. He panted as he tiptoed into the empty office. Interesting that there wasn't a drop of blood.

Maybe they only put the guy to sleep.

On the desk was a computer, stacks of paper, and a letter on stationary with the logo, "Johnson & Helms." The address on the letterhead was in a city called Hidden Falls, Indiana.

Thor fumbled with the computer thumb drive stored in his collar. He unsnapped the clasp and took the device in his mouth and awkwardly shoved the data seeker into the slot at the side of the computer. He scrolled and clicked with his paw until the info began the process of transferring onto the drive. File after file loaded as he read their content and understood what was happening to the dogs and who was behind the pandemic.

His mind worked like a computer. Although he was a dog, he was also a machine, capable of memorizing megabytes of data. The team needed the thumb drive, but he was curious. He wanted to read the data as it loaded.

The screen flashed the names and faces of people, people he had seen before, people he never expected to be involved, people in the government. His paws trembled at the significance of the data, at how this flash drive could put them behind bars forever.

The name of a drug appeared with a flow chart of how the drug, when combined with an ingredient from a dog's bone marrow, would make old people young again. He gasped. *So that's why they needed the dogs.*

But why did they have to kill them?

Thor watched several more screens, organizing the data in his computer-geeked brain, copying the data into his memory, and understanding what was happening.

While he waited for the data to transfer, he crossed the room to the file cabinets, searching for more clues. But as he opened the drawer, footsteps approached. He ducked under the desk and drew his tail in. His heart pounded so loudly he thought the person would hear it.

A man with a pair of large, shiny, black wing-tipped shoes walked to the file cabinet, the one Thor had left open. The drawer clattered and paper files shuffled. The man sighed, then paused, inhaling loudly. He sneezed once. Then again. And again.

The man spun around. "Where are you, you filthy mutt? I know you're here somewhere."

Thor tried to tuck himself tighter under the desk, but it was no use. He was too big. The man took a few steps toward him, bent his head under the desk and met Thor's eyes.

Thor stared into a set of deep muddy eyes that he had never seen before.

"I heard you were coming." The man grinned and drew his gun, pointing the barrel at the dog.

He knew I was coming? Thor bared his teeth, growled low, and lunged at the man's ankles, knocking him over, but not before the gun went off, the bullet piercing the dog's side.

Thor yelped and hobbled out the door. Burning pain seared his flesh.

The man scrambled on the floor, rubbing the back of his head.

As Thor descended the steps into the factory, sticky blood oozed from his side.

The factory workers paused to watch, their mouths gaping wide.

The man with the gun shouted from the balcony. "Stop that dog."

Workers hesitated.

Thor moved in zigzagged bursts, partially because of the pain and partially because he knew it would be more difficult for the man to shoot him again. He followed the path to where he'd entered the building and blasted through the door leading to outside, knocking down the truck driver wheeling the carcass cart.

Mindia, with wide eyes, stood immediately outside the factory's exit and pointed to the stairs leading out of the invisible spacecraft. "Hurry."

Thor inhaled sharply, bounded up the stairs, and flung himself into the invisible craft, gasping and writhing in pain. "I didn't get … the thumb drive … but I know—"

Darkness engulfed him and he fell unconscious before he could tell Mindia the rest.

CHAPTER TWO

Wily Coldren couldn't hide anywhere—especially on the school bus. He concentrated on blending in, not making a sound or drawing attention to himself, but it didn't seem to matter. Matt and Taylor, two fifth-graders from Wily's class, always seemed to find him.

The bus bounced toward Wily's street. Maybe he'd make it home without a jab. *If those jerks put one dirty finger on my glasses I'm going to … what?* He wouldn't retaliate. He never did.

Katey Prichard sat huddled in the seat across from Wily, tears streaming down her face. He wasn't sure why she was crying, but he hated seeing her sad. He reached into the front pouch of his backpack where his mom stuffed his tissues and plucked one out. When the bus stopped in front of Mrs. Flannigan's house, his bus stop, Wily stood to go and juggled his backpack. As he stood, he handed Katey the tissue.

"Thank you," she said and blotted her tears.

Wily continued down the center aisle. When he reached Matt and Taylor's seat, Matt poked Wily's side.

"Look at the blubber wiggle," Matt said.

Taylor laughed, reached over, and swiped his wet finger across Wily's glasses.

"Taylor," Mrs. Harp, the bus driver with eyes behind her back, said, "keep your backside in the seat and your hands to yourself, or I'm going to slap you with a detention."

Matt snickered.

Wily ignored them, took his glasses off, and descended the steps.

"Have a good day, Wily," Mrs. Harp said.

"You too, Mrs. Harp."

As the bus rattled past him and down the street, Wily paused at the curb, his vision blurry. He wiped his glasses with the bottom of his shirt. When he returned them to his nose he saw Mrs. Flannigan, his neighbor, heading toward him, carrying her limp poodle in her arms, tears streaming down her cheeks. She wore a flowered dress, and several pink curlers dangled from her gray-haired head.

He met her at the curbside, his stomach knotting, already suspecting what had happened to her dog. "What's wrong, Mrs. Flannigan?"

"Pookie's dead. Just like that." She hiccupped a sob. "He was running around chasing his ball this morning and then, boom, all of a sudden he keeled over and quit breathing."

Wily had heard that's how it was happening. All across the United States, dogs were dying in droves and scientists couldn't figure out why. A canine pandemic. Poor Mrs. Flannigan. Pookie was like a kid to her. The dog was all she had.

"I'm sorry. Is there something I can do?"

"The city government folks are coming to get him. They say we have to turn him in." Her sobs grew louder and tears dripped off her red nose. "They're … going to … burn him, aren't they?"

Wily gulped. He'd heard the same thing, but wasn't sure if it was true.

"They said the dogs will contaminate us, but I think they're lying. I haven't heard of one human getting sick, have you?"

"No, but maybe they're being cautious. If you want, I'll dig a hole in your yard, and you can bury him there."

"You'd do that for me?" She wiped her face with a wadded tissue.

"Sure." He glanced at his house. His mom's car was in the

driveway, which meant she was working at home, typical for a Friday. She probably wouldn't like him getting close to the dog, but if he hurried she might not have time to tell him no.

Mrs. Flannigan stopped crying. "But I already called the crew to pick him up. They'll be here any minute. What would I say to them?"

"I could tell them that they have the wrong address."

"No, I don't want you to lie for me. That wouldn't be right."

"Okay. Maybe you could give him a memorial service."

She nodded, gazing down at her dog, petting his curly hair. "Thank you. You're such a good boy, Wily. I hope you don't lose Sport."

Sport was Wily's boxer. He hoped Sport was immune to the disease.

A white truck with a booming muffler gyrated around the corner, flashed toward them, and then slowed as it approached.

Mrs. Flannigan's cries began again as she stroked Pookie's face.

"Here, give me Pookie," Wily said. "You don't want to see this." He reached for the dog and scooped the cooling body into his arms. "Go on and run in the house. I'll have Mom call you."

"Thank … you." She shuffled up the driveway in her purple slippers, her wretched cries continuing.

Wily waited for the driver to put the truck in park.

A brown-haired man in a white T-shirt, black gloves, and jeans climbed out. "Hey, kid." He walked to the back of the delivery truck and lifted the door, its wheels squealing and clanking as they rolled.

Wily followed the man and peered into the truck. Dogs of all sizes and breeds—boxers like Sport, Labs, schnauzers, wiener dogs, short-haired and long-haired ones, were stacked one on top of the other. Flies buzzed around them. The stench made him gag. He held Pookie closer. "Where are you taking them?"

"To the drop-off site."

"Where's that?"

"What's it to you? Hand over the dead dog and go take a shower. You're contaminated now."

Wily didn't trust he guy, but didn't know what else to do. He wished he could follow him to where he was taking the animals, to see exactly what was happening, but he was only eleven, too young to drive. Reluctantly, he handed Pookie over, promising himself to find out more and learn where the dogs were going.

The man tossed Pookie in the back like a sack of trash. He shut the door, and climbed in the truck, the wheels grinding in rhythm, Pookie nothing more than a memory.

Wily's head hung low as the truck pulled away.

#

About an hour later, wearing his protective eye gear, Wily bent over the kitchen counter in his suburban Indiana home. He peered intently at the dead frog on the board next to his voltage meter and prepared to connect the wires. He had worked for months on galvanism, a way to use electricity to stimulate life. Frankenstein had done it, so maybe there was a way he could too.

What if he could bring the dying dogs back to life?

Sport lay on the cold tile beside him, occasionally glancing at Wily as if he knew the clock was ticking, that if Wily didn't find an answer soon, Sport would be shipped off to who-knows-where, like Pookie and the rest of the dead dogs.

Wily's mom stood a few feet away, sautéing cauliflower in olive oil. "Mrs. Flannigan called her sister, and she's coming to stay with her for a few days. It was nice of you to help her, but you have to be careful, Wily. I don't want you contracting whatever it is these dogs have."

"I'm healthy, Mom. No worries. Plus, I took a shower using that extra scratchy soap Dad likes."

"Speaking of Dad—he's on his way. We're going to eat soon. Put your stuff away."

"Aw, Mom. I'm about to prove Galvani's theory of animal electricity. I'm so close. If I can discover the electromotive force of a galvanic cell I might be able to cure dying dogs. I think my black box has all the parts now."

She reached over and messed his hair, shaking her head. "That's my boy, trying to save the world."

"No, not the world, just dogs. Don't you see? Sport might be next."

Sport let out a long snort.

His mother paused and looked at Wily first, then at Sport. "Let's hope not, honey. It's probably a weird virus. I'm sure someone will figure it out soon. Keep Sport in the house as much as possible until they figure out what's causing the problem."

"Who's going to figure it out? The scientists are looking at the wrong data." He peered over the top of his plastic safety glasses at his mom. She was a psychologist. What did she know about experiments and scientific data?

"How do you know?"

"Because I read the papers." He knelt on the floor in front of Sport, then pulled the dog's eyelid down, studied the redness, and examined the color of his whites. Something fishy was going on in the world. Why would the government order people to send their dead animals to a central location, loading them onto trucks like garbage? He doubted the dead dogs were a hazard to people. Maybe something else was going on. "I wish you'd let me use my invention, Mom. Please? Just once so I can see if it works."

"No, it's too risky, not until we have a professor from Oakland Tech look it over. I don't want you to burn down the house or get electrocuted." His mother returned to the stove. "I know you mean well, but I'm sure this whole matter is more complicated than you realize." She stole a glance out the window. "You better get your stuff out of here. Your dad won't like to see your science lab in the kitchen, so clean it up, and you can work on it later."

"All right. Give me two more seconds." Wily hooked the wires to the frog's legs. "What's for dinner?"

"Cauliflower and chickpea stew with couscous."

Huh? "It smells awesome." His stomach growled. He loved food almost as much as conducting experiments. He scribbled his progress on the data chart and graph next to the frog and reconnected the wires one last time. He was so engrossed in his work he didn't realize his father had entered the room until a large hand clamped his shoulder.

Wily startled. The wires brushed against each other causing a spark and sending a jolt up his arm.

His dad flinched and shouted, "What the— Are you trying to burn down the house?"

"Sorry, Dad. I was finishing my research. Did you see the news today? More dogs are dying. If I can find a way to stimulate cell activity, I might have the solution to save them."

His father wrinkled his nose as he looked over Wily's shoulder at the experiment board. "I can't believe you have a slime infested frog within a few feet of my dinner. Put that stuff away before you contaminate us or blow up the kitchen."

Why couldn't his dad believe him for once? Why couldn't he trust that Wily knew what he was doing?

His dad reached for his mom who stood over the stove combining the chickpeas with the sauce. He pulled her into a hug, kissing the back of her neck. "Smells good, but not as good as you. I bet it won't taste as good either."

Disgusting. Why couldn't his dad nibble on her in the other room?

Mom giggled. "Oh, you. Stop. Go wash your hands so we can eat." She shooed him away with the kitchen towel.

Wily took his supplies and carried them to the table in his bedroom where he stored the boxes of wires, voltage meters, and his other electrical inventions.

CHAPTER THREE

After dinner, Wily sat with his parents at the table.

His dad grinned. "I got you something for your birthday."

Wily leaned in. "Is it a new microscope?"

His dad's eyes shone brightly. "No, this is something more fun."

What could be more fun than a new high-powered scope? "Is it the new thermoelectric tool kit on page twenty-two of the *American Science and Surplus* catalog?"

His father shook his head and squeezed his brows together.

"Is it the new high voltage meter?"

"No, this is something we can do together." He flashed a smile at Wily's mom. "I saw Scott Feldman today."

"Who's that?" Wily asked.

His father shook his head. "I have to verse you on who's who in the major leagues, son. Scott Feldman is the Chicago Cubs pitcher." Wily's dad had played major league football. He knew everyone who was anyone in sports.

"What does he have to do with my birthday?" Wily asked.

"He gave me two tickets in the best seats at Wrigley Field." He pulled out his wallet and threw the two tickets onto the table.

Wily stared at them, smiled, and tried to look interested. "Oh, that's great, Dad."

"The game is Saturday," his dad said.

"But Saturday is the Electrical Science Fair at Oakland Tech. Mom's taking me to present my invention." He looked over at his mom as she stacked the dirty dishes on the table.

"He's right, Ben. I did tell him that I'd take him." She turned to Wily. "But maybe you could go to the one in the fall at Purdue instead."

Wily huffed. He'd have to wait months before he'd know if his box worked. But he couldn't disappoint his dad. "Okay." He picked up his plate and put it in the dishwasher, his shoulders drooping.

"What? You're not going to act even a little happy?" his dad asked.

Wily caught sight of his mother's frown.

"I'm happy, Dad." He lied. "It'll be a good time." The only good part of a boring baseball game was the hot dogs and popcorn. All the rest was a waste of time.

Sport followed Wily to the pantry like he always did after supper.

The dog food bag crinkled in Wily's grasp. He poured the nuggets into the bowl and they dinged on the bottom.

Sport sniffed the chicken and sweet potato formula, wrinkled his nose, and walked away.

Oh, no! Typically, he wolfed down his dinner.

"You okay, boy?" Wily asked.

Sport sat beside Wily, not interested in eating.

Wily pointed toward the food. "Go ahead and eat."

Sport wouldn't budge.

Maybe he was saving it for later. Wily shrugged and turned to go.

Sport followed Wily down the hallway and into his bedroom. He jumped up onto the bed and rested his head on his paws.

Willy plopped into his desk chair, then faced Sport, and patted the dog's head, lifting his eyelids one at a time again. The dog's eyes appeared the same as they always had.

Sport licked Wily's hand.

"You have an upset stomach?"

The dog barked.

Maybe Sport had eaten something down at the pond today—a dead fish. He'd done that before. Sport would probably wake up puking in the middle of the night and then want to eat. Yeah, that was probably the problem.

Wily reached for his iPad on the desk. *I wonder when Purdue's science fair is?* He clicked the space bar to Google the information.

His parents' voices trickled in from the kitchen. He hadn't meant to leave his door ajar, but he had. It was open just enough to hear his parents argue. Again.

"You need to enroll him in some exercise classes. He's getting fatter," his father said. "And how's he ever going to learn social skills if he's cooped up in the house working on an *insane* black box?"

"Oh, Ben. That's who he is. He doesn't want to be an athlete like you."

"That's obvious. But he's too soft," his dad said. "He's too nice to those kids who make fun of him. He's weak, Bridget. It's going to get him into trouble. He'll never learn how to stand up for himself if you keep babying him."

He was too soft? Too weak?

"Shhh," his mom said. "He's going to hear you."

CHAPTER FOUR

Wily covered his ears. He didn't want to hear his parents anymore. This argument wouldn't be any different than the others. He stood, moved to the window and opened it, then heaved Sport into his arms, and climbed out. After he set Sport on the earth, Wily closed the sash behind him.

Today had been an unusually warm spring day. His shirt clung to him, reminding him of why he didn't like to spend time outdoors. But at least the days were getting longer and the sun was still shining. He hiked past the budding maple trees and toward the gurgling stream that bordered the edge of their five acres. The pond, his favorite place to be alone with nature, was filled with his frog specimens.

Squirrels chattered, birds called, and bees buzzed, but halfway to the water, Sport sneezed, snorted, and coughed repeatedly. His tail tucked between his legs.

Wily dropped to his knees and took the dog's head in his hands, panic fisting his heart. "What is it, boy?"

But he knew.

The dog's tongue hung crooked out of his mouth as he panted. A long whooshing noise escaped from his nostrils and he teetered to the earth.

"No!" Wily dropped to his knees.

Sport whined and gazed up at Wily with panic-stricken eyes. His lids closed as if he were too weak to keep them open. His chest rose and fell rapidly.

Wily had to save him.

"It's okay, buddy. I'm here." Wily scooped Sport in his arms and grunted as he stood. "Steady." He started back toward the house, one short step at a time, perspiration trickling down his back.

When he reached his bedroom window, he set the dog on the ground and lifted the sash. Then he hoisted the dog up and in through the window.

By this time Sport's breathing had quickened.

"Hang on, Buddy."

Wily climbed into the room and closed the window, then bent to lift Sport onto the table. The dog's body was limp, with no air escaping from his mouth.

Sport's eyes rolled up under his lids and he stopped breathing.

"No." Wily reached for the black box in his closet. He couldn't wait. It was now or never. He didn't have time to ask for permission. This might be Sport's only chance. The sticky padded electrodes with the wired ends were already connected to the terminal ends on his box, so all he had to do was fasten the pads to Sport's chest and head.

Tears blurred his vision. When everything was in place, he hesitated over the ON switch, doubt filling him. Would it work or would it fail— and fry Sport? Fear of failure crawled under his skin, burning inside him.

He squeezed the tears out of his eyes. *I have to try.*

He flipped the switch.

Nothing.

He flipped the switch off and then flipped it back on. "Come back, guy. You have to come back." He cried.

Sport's body began to glow. Faintly.

Wily paused, exhaling slowly, and then sucked in a breath, not sure if his eyes were playing tricks on him. He blinked and wiped them with the back of his arm.

Sport changed from a golden color, to red, then he glowed as white as the moon on a dark night.

Wily gasped. The light was too bright for his eyes. His knees buckled and he gripped the edge of the table to keep from collapsing.

Sport's eyelids fluttered. His pupils were no longer rolled up under his lids, but instead were fixed on Wily. A sharp, quick breath escaped from the dog's tongue-drooping mouth.

"What the—?" Wily took a step back.

The white glow faded. His room stilled. Sport's eyes closed again.

Wily went to the dog, hunkered over him, and pressed a hand on the dog's heart. He had a faint beat.

Sport stretched and rolled onto his side.

Wily shrieked at the sudden movement, backing up to stand a foot away.

Sport opened his eyes. He gathered his feet beneath him and leaped off the table, the wires tearing from the machines and dangling from his head and chest. He barked and licked Wily's hand with his slobbery tongue.

Wily knelt with his mouth open wide, taking Sport in his arms and rubbing his ears. "It worked, boy. It worked." He shook his head as if he were dreaming. He'd actually figured out the way to save dogs, to bring them back to life.

Sport barked again and lunged toward Wily playfully, darting and running in circles.

Wily stroked the dog's back, then stood stunned. The electronic gizmo sat on his desk, clunky and dark, but it had worked. "Mom. I did it." His heart raced as he threw open his door and ran out of his bedroom, heading toward the living room.

Sport followed, panting and prancing.

"Mom."

A TV newscaster's voice sounded from the living room. Wily followed the sound, breathing hard.

His mother and father were sitting on the sofa watching TV.

His mother faced him. "What's wrong?"

"You … aren't going … to believe … this." He panted between the words.

"Believe what?" she asked.

His father lifted his arm. "Shhh, they're going to announce the scores. Can you talk in the other room?" He grabbed the remote and raised the volume, his eyes glued to the TV.

"Sport keeled over." Wily pointed toward his room. "And I healed him. I saved him, Mom. He was barely breathing, and well," he took a few deep breaths, "and he died, but I brought him back to life."

His mother stared at Wily, her mouth agape. "Oh." She glanced at the dog. "You used him in an experiment?" Then she shot a glance toward Wily's dad.

His father threw up his hands. "See what I mean, Bridget? See what you've done?"

"What *I've* done? What are you talking about? I didn't *do* anything." His mother's voice was an octave higher than usual. She shook her head at Wily. "Why don't you get ready for bed? I think you're tired."

"No, Mom. Really. It happened. I used my invention."

She pointed a finger at him. "That heap of metal you promised not to touch?"

Wily paused. "Yes, but Mom, Sport was dead. I had to try."

His dad muted the TV. "Did you disobey your mother?"

Wily dropped his head.

His mother stood, came around the back of the sofa, and put her hand on Wily's forehead. "Maybe we need to take the box away so the temptation isn't so great." She walked toward the hall.

Wily followed. "You don't believe me, do you?"

She stopped in front of his door. "I want to believe you, honey, but I think if electricity could save a dog's life someone would have discovered that already."

"I swear. Sport was really dead."

"Don't swear." She walked past him and entered his room that smelled of singed hair. Wrinkling her nose, she lifted the black box off the table and left the room. On her way to the laundry room to hide the box, she said over her shoulder, "I bought some pistachio ice cream today. How about a bowl?"

Wily frowned.

"He doesn't need ice cream, he needs a workout routine," his father hollered.

Sport dashed to his food bowl and devoured the contents, smacking his chops and slurping his water.

Shortly after, Wily lay in his bed with an empty ice cream bowl at his side, unable to sleep. He stared at the TV on his dresser, watching his favorite movie, *Avatar*. He loved the movie because the hero, Jake Sully, started out as nobody but became somebody to the people of Pandora.

Wily fell asleep wishing he could be that kind of hero, someone so important that people would notice him, believe him, and maybe like him, someone his dad would respect.

Had he imagined that he'd brought Sport back to life?

No, it had really happened.

CHAPTER FIVE

Wily woke early with a start. The sun's bright face peeked in through the slats of the blinds and onto Sport, revealing the gentle rise and fall of his chest. He still seemed okay. The dog slept with his head burrowed under a pillow at the foot of Wily's bed—as he often did, like nothing had changed.

Wily climbed out of bed in his plaid pajamas, went to the window, opened the blind, and looked into the backyard through the trees. The morning would be cool enough to hunt for frogs, but he didn't feel like conducting experiments. What was the point? Besides, it was Saturday and his dad would be home and wouldn't want to have frogs in the house.

A cardinal flew across the yard to the bird feeder, perched on the peg, and plucked a seed from the hole. It's red feathers a sharp contrast against the brush of the budding green trees.

Wily sighed. Even though life around him seemed the same, inside he felt different. He'd invented something that would change the world, but his own parents didn't believe him.

He moseyed into his closet, stepped into his slippers, and patted his thigh. "Come on, Sport."

The dog followed him out of the bedroom, down the hallway, and into the laundry room. Before he reached the side door, he spotted his box on the shelf above the dryer, locked inside a glass cabinet, like all his other *forbidden* treasures. Wily paused and sighed. "It did save you, didn't it, boy? You know the truth."

The dog barked.

"Shhh." Thank goodness his parents slept on the other side of the house. Wily's parents would stay in bed until at least ten, which was fine with him. It would give him time to sort through what he was going to do next.

Wily let Sport out the door and retrieved the morning paper lying on the porch. On his way to the kitchen, he unfolded the paper and read the headline: "Animal Scientists Puzzled as Thousands More Die."

He set the paper on the kitchen table and went to the pantry, but as he was about to reach for the box of Lucky Charms, a knock sounded at the side door—the same door he'd been at—the one in the laundry room. He paused to listen again. Sport? No, Sport took his time in the morning, meandering down to the stream, chasing squirrels. It couldn't be him.

Tap, tap, tap.

No, this was a faint knock. He set the cereal on the counter and headed to the door. Who would be coming to the house at this hour and knocking at the side door? People typically used the front door.

When he opened the door, a girl about his age smiled at him. She had blond hair pulled back in a pale blue headband. The blue was the same color as her eyes. He'd never seen her before.

"Hi, I'm Mindia. You need to come with me because the entire dog race is at stake."

Was she from Mars? Wily closed his eyes, shook his head, and opened his eyes again. Yep, the girl still stood there, her pale eyes intensely piercing his, making absolutely no sense.

"Uh, I think you have the wrong house. Who exactly are you looking for?"

"I have the right house, Wily. We need you."

She knew his name? Who was the *we* she referred to?

"We saw the way you healed Sport yesterday."

Huh? "You saw me?" He glanced out in the yard over her shoulder, to her right, then to her left. Were there others lurking nearby? His heart fluttered, and he started to shut the door, but the girl slid her foot over the threshold.

"Wait," she said. Her eyes lit up with blue spirals of light.

He stared at her as if she was from outer space and pressed the door shut with all his might, but it wouldn't budge.

The freaky girl stared at him with her intense eyes.

He paused. Something about her stare made him unable to look away. He was under her spell. She was taking control of his mind.

"Where is your black box?" she asked.

"In the cabinet," Wily said.

"Get it and bring it here," she said.

Wily nodded, but first he needed his Swiss Army knife to unlock the cabinet. He absent-mindedly shuffled to his bedroom, opened his desk drawer, and grabbed the knife. When he returned to the laundry room, the girl was still there, waiting.

Wily hopped on top of the dryer, opened the awl blade on the knife, shoved its pointy tip into the lock, and jiggled the blade. Instantly, the cabinet opened. Wily reached up, snatched the box, and jumped down.

"Follow me," the girl said. "And bring your box."

Wily wanted to say, no, or wait, at least let me change out of my baggy pajamas, or let me get my dog, but he couldn't utter a word. The girl's brain was talking to his brain and telling him what to do. He couldn't resist her. He slipped the Swiss knife into the little pocket of his PJs.

"I'm sorry to have to do it this way, but I don't have a choice right now," she said. "We're in a hurry."

Wily nodded, glued to her spinning eyeballs. "No problem."

What? Did he say that?

Holding his black box, he took a step toward her.

She took his arm, hers small and warm.

He followed her out, closing the door behind him and shuffling along in his moccasin slippers.

She led him along the path at the south end of his property and out into the side street, the one at the end of their driveway. Suddenly something hissed, and a set of metal stairs descended out of thin air. A narrow door swooshed open at the top of the stairs.

An older boy of about fourteen appeared. "Hi, Wily. That's cool that you decided to help us. I'm Devon, the pilot of this shuttle." He extended his hand.

Wily juggled the black box and shook Devon's hand. *Had he decided to help them? And how did this kid know his name too? And what shuttle was he talking about?*

"You can't see our shuttle yet, but once you climb aboard you'll know what I'm talking about," Devon said. "Here, let me help you with that." Devon reached for the box.

Wily handed Devon the box. *Was he dreaming?* He pinched his own arm. "Ouch." Nope.

Devon nodded for Wily to climb the stairs that led to nowhere.

Mindia stood to the side, her eyes still glued to Wily's.

Wily hesitated. He shouldn't go. These were strangers. He didn't know anything about these kids, but Mindia placed her hand on his arm and met his eyes again. The spinning blue circles continued, hypnotizing him deeper.

"Okay." He nodded and stepped up.

Mindia and Devon followed him.

Once Wily stepped beyond the door, he entered a glass-bubble shuttle the size of a large van. The craft hovered about two feet above the ground. It had no wheels and made soft swishing noises.

The door shut with another hiss.

Wily spun around. He was trapped.

Mindia motioned for him to take a seat, her eyes finally stopping their spiraling motion. "I'm sorry I had to take control of your mind, but it was important that you come with us. I didn't have time to explain." She spoke softly, her voice a feather floating in the air.

"Who are you and where are you taking me?" Wily asked. His heart thudded, his stomach swirled, his mouth went dry, and the reality that he was tricked into a hovercraft with strangers clawed at reality. Nothing was normal here.

CHAPTER SIX

The flying craft jerked and then glided, floating through the air, jolting Wily into his seat. The air smelled of dust and electrical wire from all the computer electronics at the control board.

Mindia sat next to him. "We're going to base. It shouldn't take long to get there. Doctor Doobig will explain everything." She reached for Wily's hand and squeezed it. "Don't be scared. We won't hurt you." She gazed at him with a dreamy expression.

Weird. His cheeks heated. No girl had looked at him that way, touched his hand so tenderly, or spoke to him in such a caring way. It felt creepy.

He flung his hand out of hers and shot out of the seat, his backside banging on the side glass. "Let me out of here." The spacecraft dipped and shuddered, knocking him to the floor.

Devon, who sat at the front of the shuttle with the controls, turned to Wily. "Cool it. You're going to crash this thing."

"How am I supposed to stay calm when I'm being abducted by aliens?"

Devon laughed, keeping his head forward as he navigated the craft in front of him, "We aren't aliens. We're kids, the same as you, that's all."

How were they anything like him?

Wily's knees trembled, but he didn't want these kids to think he was as afraid as he felt. Better to stay calm. That's what he did in school when the bullies threatened him. He brushed his hands on his pants, stood, and shook a strand of hair out of his eyes. He returned to the seat across from Mindia.

Devon pushed a few buttons.

Wily swallowed hard. He stared through the glass at the bottom of the craft while they traveled over treetops and rooftops, low enough for Wily to recognize where they were. They passed Billy's house, his mom's office, and their church. He choked at the bile rising in his throat. Rides had never been his thing. Saliva pooled in his mouth.

"You'll feel better if you look out instead of down," Mindia said. "Motion sickness is common the first time you ride."

"I feel fine." Wily looked out instead. Mr. Keller, his science teacher, walked his poodle. Wily banged on the window. "Mr. Keller. Help."

"He can't see you," Mindia said. "We're invisible to him like we were with you."

"How?" Wily asked, swallowing loudly.

"We use metamaterials," Devon said over his shoulder. "It's the same sort of thing used in disappearing cloaks, only we use it over this craft and home base too."

"*Base?*"

"Our home. It's hovering over Costco," Mindia said.

Costco? "How long have you been there?"

Mindia shrugged. "I've been here for eight years, but others have been there longer."

"Others? How many?" Wily wiped his sweaty palms on his PJ bottoms.

"Too many to count," Devon said. "It's a fairly large community of geeks." He laughed.

"Geeks?"

"Yeah, kids like you, me, Mindia. Kids with special powers who can help change the world," Devon said.

"Kids with *powers*? I don't have powers."

Mindia giggled and slipped her hand into Wily's again. "Yes, you do. We saw what you did with Sport."

What? That was the second time she'd said that. And why did she have to keep taking his hand? He slowly released it. "Wh … what … do you … mean? Were you peeking into my window or something?"

Mindia and Devon exchanged glances.

Devon chuckled. "No, we didn't have to be looking through your window to see *your* rays."

"Rays?"

Devon nodded toward a monitor. "See that screen there?"

Wily nodded, observing a twelve-inch screen displaying aerial views of homes, stores, and schools, the picture constantly shifting to reveal a different location. Some homes had yellow flashes of light jetting from them.

"We have several of those monitors at base, only they're much larger," Devon said. "When a kid has powers, the screen shows an electromagnetic energy different than others. The monitors are our detection system. See the yellow lights coming from here?" He pointed and used a remote to freeze the screen. "A kid with powers lives there, so we observe him, but his light is dim. Chances are he'll outgrow his powers or it could be a while before he's ready. Your rays started out brighter than anyone else's we've seen. Yesterday they lit up the whole sky."

"But I don't have powers. All I have is a black box." He pointed to the contraption that Devon had placed on the floor near the door.

Devon's eyebrows shot up. "Well, whatever is in that box is powerful."

Wily puffed out his chest feeling proud that these strangers believed him.

"That's normal—for parents to diss their kids," Mindia said. "Parents rarely understand."

Huh? How did she know what he'd been thinking?

Mindia stared out the window, seemingly lost in thought.

Was it his imagination or was Mindia reading his mind? No, that wasn't possible. "Look, I don't have powers. I'm a normal kid who happens to like experiments." And he didn't like how these kids had spied on him.

Mindia nodded to him. "I know all this might sound creepy, but we don't pry into your personal life or spy on you. It's just that we watch for the kids who can help. We have a purpose. We've been waiting to confront you and now we couldn't wait any longer."

"Waiting to confront me? But how can *I* help *you?*" Before they had a chance to answer, Wily saw base on Devon's screen. Wily let out a long whistle. It was like something out of a Star Wars movie, a huge metal space ship with sharp angular lines floated about a hundred feet above Costco. As if it were stalking the store. How had he never seen it before?

Wily peered through the windshield of the craft. Base was no where in sight. He glanced at Devon's screen again. There it was. He scanned back and forth, up and down. The ship was on the screen, but not visible through the windshield.

"It's only visible using the technology through the monitor," Mindia said. "You're seeing it now because, for now, you're a part of the team."

"Team? What team?" And how did she know what he was thinking all the time?

She touched his arm. "I'm sorry I'm intruding in on your thoughts. That's rude. I'll try not to, okay? I've spent a lifetime knowing what people are thinking. It's only recently I learned how to shut it off, but I'm not good at it yet. I'll try." She closed her eyes as if concentrating.

She *had* known his thoughts. Wily nodded, stopping himself from saying what he really thought—that she was weird.

"Not so fast, Mindia" Devon interrupted. "Before we mention joining our team, we have to make sure he'll help us."

Wily's body stiffened. "How?"

"You'll see. Soon." Mindia winked.

Wily wiped his sweaty palms on his pajama bottoms again. That's what he was afraid of—what he would see and what it would mean to be a part of their team. He had a sinking feeling it meant doing something dangerous, something he had never done before.

CHAPTER SEVEN

The craft jostled slightly, then clinked as it locked beneath the larger craft. Wily's heart pounded fast in his chest.

Devon pushed a few buttons and scooted out from his seat. He walked to the door and pushed another button. The door opened with the familiar hiss revealing a long blue-lit hallway.

Wily followed Mindia down the stairs and out of the craft. Devon retrieved Wily's box and followed.

An older boy, about sixteen, greeted them. He had dark hair curling over his ears, brown eyes—normal, non-spiraling eyes—and wore jeans and a T-shirt. He extended his hand to Wily and smirked, eyeing his clothes. "Nice jammies there, Wily."

He knew his name too? "I didn't exactly have time to change." Wily gave the guy his hand.

"Yeah, sorry about that. It couldn't be helped. Thanks for coming. I'm Lucky." He headed down the hallway and motioned for Wily, Mindia, and Devon to follow.

Was he lucky to have Wily here? Or was his name Lucky?

"His name is Lucky," Mindia whispered in Wily's ear.

There she goes again.

Lucky took wide steps down the hall. "Hurry. There isn't much time."

"Much time for what?" Wily asked, hesitating as he followed.

Lucky spoke over his shoulder. "To help Thor. If you don't save him, all the dogs in the world will continue to die."

Wily gasped, digging his heels in and pausing in his tracks. "What?"

Mindia threaded her arm through Wily's, coaxing him forward. "Follow us. We'll show you."

A sour blob hung in the back of Wily's throat. He didn't have a good feeling about this.

Rows of rectangular florescent lights lit the blue-carpeted hallway and cast a blue hue onto the stark white walls. A sweet aroma, like Juicy Fruit chewing gum, filled the air and made Wily's stomach rumble with hunger. What an idiot. How could he think about food at a time like this?

The ceiling was a brushed silver metallic as were the doorknobs. The group passed several closed doors until they came to the end of the hallway. Devon followed from behind, still holding the box.

Lucky opened the door to a room and held it for the rest of them to enter. "Good luck. I'll catch you guys later. I'm needed in the lab." He shut the door as he left.

Wily stood frozen in the middle of the room that resembled a hospital emergency room complete with a bed, sink, and cabinets.

Lying on a gurney was the largest black Great Dane Wily had ever seen. The dog's eyes were shut, a plastic tube protruded from a mask on his face, and bandages covered his abdomen. A machine beeped at his side.

An older man with wiry brown hair and super long feet, and wearing a red lab coat said, "Finally. It's nice to meet you, Wily."

He knows me too?

"I'm Dr. Doobig. You know, the opposite of Dr. Doolittle. Do big." He laughed at his attempt at a joke. "Our dog, Thor, needs your help." He rested his hand on Wily's shoulder and squeezed.

Devon placed Wily's box on the end of the gurney near the dog and scooted a chair beside him. He petted Thor's ear.

The dog didn't budge.

"What can *I* do?" Wily said.

The doctor patted Wily's back. "You, my boy, can bring him back to life. He's been shot. He's basically dead except for these machines keeping him alive, but not for long."

Wily backed up. "You've got the wrong guy. I can't save him." Wily's feet sweated in his moccasins.

"You can do it," Doc said. "You give off more glowing rays than any other healer this side and that side of Costco."

"But I've only saved my dog, and, er, with electricity. It's not *my* powers. It's science."

Mindia squeezed his arm. He'd forgotten she was still at his side. She must have known that he wanted to run. Far.

"W-w-what if it doesn't work?"

The room grew silent except for the beeping of the machines. The doctor's eyebrows raised, creasing his forehead. "You have to try." He took Wily's hands and led him toward Thor's still body. "Tell us what you need and we'll get you everything. This is for Thor's life, but also for all the dogs in America."

The door to the hallway burst open.

"Wait." The tallest, darkest, most spidery-looking woman with a horse's body stood before them.

Wily gasped. He'd only seen centaurs and centaurides in mythology books. They didn't exist. He closed his eyes, shook his head, and opened his eyes again. The creature was still there.

She had long, dark hair to her waist and wide, green, cat eyes. Her skin had a milky appearance, but it was her four long slender legs, two arms, and pointed black fingernails that got his attention. Strips of black fabric dangled from her arms, giving her an eight-legged spider look. But her back half was the body of a horse. She half trotted and half slinked toward them. "Did you tell him what could happen?"

Dr. Doobig crossed the room and faced the woman, blocking her path to Wily. "Get out. Don't complicate things." He waved his hand at her.

She stepped around the doc and faced Wily, so close he could smell her—a mixture of the vanilla his mom used in sugar cookies and sap from pine trees. An odd combined scent.

He shuddered and took a step back.

She folded her arms across her chest and leaned back, staring squarely into Wily's eyes. "I think he has a right to know. It's not fair to put him in this situation without giving him all the facts."

Wily froze. "What facts?" He licked his lips.

She continued her stare. Even her eyelashes were long and spindly. "If you save Thor, the Dark Horse will make you stay here. Forever. You'll never be free again."

"The Dark Horse?" Wily heaved a heavy breath and flashed a look toward Doc and Mindia. Then he turned back to Spider Woman. He didn't know who the Dark Horse was, but he didn't sound friendly.

The spider woman nodded. "You'll be bound to this ship like the rest of us here." She motioned to the others in the room.

"You mean I'll never see my family again?" Wily asked.

"Sure you will, son," said Dr. Doobig, sliding his glasses back up on his nose. "From up here though." He gestured toward the city below. "Not from down there."

Wily trembled. "Oh. I'm sorry ... but ... I can't ... help you. Please take me home." He hated himself for sounding like a wuss, but was scared to think he'd never see his parents again. He moved to the door.

"Wait," Dr. Doobig said. "If you don't help Thor, we might never know who's behind this mass murder."

Wily stopped, his hand on the doorknob. "Mass murder?"

"All the dogs in the world will die," Doc said. "It's already started."

But Wily knew, and hadn't he told his mom he wanted to find a way to save the dogs? "How will saving Thor help the rest of the dogs?"

The doctor leaned against the examining table. "Thor is the only one who can lead us to the person who's behind all this. If he dies we'll never know, and by the time we figure it out, it'll be too late. Dogs will become extinct."

Wily's eyes grew larger. No more Sport? No more dogs? "How can that be possible?" *Could he live with himself knowing he could have prevented the canine pandemic?* "Why would someone do this?"

"Greed. Money. It's always about money," Doc said. "Only Thor knows the details. He got shot before he could tell us what he found."

"Tell you? What, is he going to speak in English?" Wily laughed, nervously, but no one else laughed.

Spider centaur woman raised her eyebrows and smirked at Doc.

"Thor knows how to communicate with Mindia," Doc said, clearing his throat. "She can read his thoughts."

Mindia nodded, lifting her shoulders a little straighter.

This was getting weirder by the minute. He shook his head as if he could shake a dream away.

Doc, Mindia, Devon, and Spider Woman gaped at him, waiting for an answer. The machines whirred.

Wily's arms trembled. "I can't help you." He dropped his head, staring at his slippers.

Spider Woman stepped forward. "I think that's a good decision. The Dark Horse might let you return if you go now, but you better hurry." She took his arm and reached to open the door.

Wily felt a second of relief. He couldn't wait to leave this all behind.

Doc moved toward Spider Woman, his brow creased, and set his hand on her arm. "You're scaring him." Then he spoke to Wily. "Look, this isn't a bad place, and we need your help. If you could do this, you'd be a hero."

A hero? Like Jake Sully? Liked by other kids? And respected as a scientist? His father had said he was weak, that his compassion would get him in trouble. Wily walked over to Thor and placed his hand on his head. The poor dog. So many others were dying too. He took a deep breath. "Let's say I could save him and he leads us to the bad guys, who says we can stop them?"

Spider Woman nodded at Dr. Doobig. "That's exactly my point. There are no guarantees here, Doc, and you know it."

The doctor sighed and glanced at Wily. "This ship is full of kids who are willing to do what it takes to capture the criminals. I believe with their powers we have the ability to do what it'll take. I have faith in our team."

"He's right," Mindia said, stepping beside Doc.

But Spider Woman's expression remained stoic.

Why was she opposed to Wily's help?

She stepped toward Doc. "If they all die then the rest of the centaurs will never return. That's our best option."

The rest of the centaurs? What did she mean by "best option"? How could the death of all the dogs be a good option?

"Yes," Doc said to the woman between clenched teeth, seeming to spit his words. "But we could kiss our lives good-bye too."

Whoa. Wait a minute. If Wily didn't help them they'd all die too? He felt like puking.

Mindia placed her warm hand in Wily's. "It's complicated, but I promise, you won't be disappointed if you help. Doing something heroic gives your life purpose."

He scanned the room, his eyes probing the eyes of the others who stared back at him, seeming to beg him, desperately. All, except Spider Woman.

Mindia appeared to hold her breath.

The clock on the wall ticked. The machines whooshed.

Wily choked on his phlegm and coughed. He'd never had to make a choice like this. He could help Thor, save the dogs, maybe save all the lives of the kids on the ship even though he didn't understand it all, and learn who the criminals were.

Or he could turn and walk away, go back home, and forget this ever happened. Forget that he may have had the power to change the course of animal history, but was too cowardly to try. If he returned home and all the dogs died, he'd have to live with the fact that he never tried to save them. He couldn't walk away. He couldn't. Maybe this was a way to do something good.

But if he never made it home no one would know that he was a hero.

But *he* would know. That was all that mattered.

He sucked in a long breath and thought of his hero, Jake Sully. He'd sacrificed his race for another. He left his home to save an entirely new people. And found happiness.

CHAPTER EIGHT

Wily's eyes shifted from the woman, to Thor, to Mindia, and rested on the doctor. "You said I could see my family from here. How?"

The doctor nodded. "There's a way. We have built-in cameras, like the ones we used to see you."

"Is getting back home impossible?" Wily said.

The doctor and the spider woman exchanged glances. The woman said, "Yes."

Dr. Doobig shook his head. "It's possible, but no one has ever done it."

She stomped her hoof. "Don't give him false hope."

"Don't be such a pessimist," Doc said to her, his face inches from hers. "We don't know what the boy is capable of."

Wily stroked the dog's ear and trembled; the pressure of the moment sat on his chest. "And what if I try to save him, but he dies anyway? What then? Will I still be locked here forever?"

"No," Doc said. "In that case you would be free to go. The Dark Horse would be angry, but he'd throw you out. He only keeps those who are helpful."

"But first he'd erase your memory," Devon said.

Throw him out? Erase his memory? That didn't sound good, but at least he wouldn't have to remember that he'd failed. "What's the food like here?" he asked Mindia.

She smiled. "Excellent. Nora is the chef. She's amazing. She has special skills to mesh and mix ingredients to create flavors you've never tasted."

Wily heaved a sigh. In the end, he couldn't walk away. He had to try to help. Maybe his father was right—his compassionate nature would be his downfall, but somewhere he learned that it was better to try than to fail from never trying at all. This was his chance to do something good, to prove his father wrong.

"Okay. I'll try to help, but don't get your hopes up. I've only done this once."

The doctor exhaled loudly and patted Wily's back. "Thank you. Believe in yourself. You'll be our hero."

That was inconceivable, but definitely desirable.

If he were never allowed to leave the ship, then nobody from home would know he'd saved the canine race. He decided he didn't care. He'd never helped others because he wanted the recognition. He'd done it because he wanted to do the right thing.

The doctor clasped Wily's arm and pulled him toward the black box at the foot of the gurney, near where Devon sat. "Go ahead. He doesn't have much time."

Wily scooted the box toward Thor's abdomen. "I need sticky pads with wires and an electrical outlet."

Mindia pointed to the wall socket. "There's one. I'll go to the lab and get the wires. What kind do you need?"

Wily rattled off the supplies he needed, then Mindia hurried out the door.

Wily made sure the switch on the box was off, then plugged the black box's cord into the outlet.

Devon chewed his nails and Doc paced. Spider Woman leaned against the wall, her arms folded across her chest.

Wily's fingers trembled and he flicked his hair out of his eyes.

The machines attached to Thor suddenly beeped, replacing the soft whooshing sounds. A red light on the monitor pulsed and a long horizontal line appeared on the screen.

What's that? Wily jerked.

"We've lost him. His heart has stopped." Doc rushed to check the machines.

Wily had to try to bring the dog back. He forced himself to think positive. The dog was officially dead now so nothing worse could happen.

Mindia rushed into the room, puffing to catch her breath. She handed Wily a container full of wires and sticky padded electrodes—all the things he'd asked for and more.

Taking the wires out of the container, he began to systematically connect them to the black box and then connect the other ends to the pads. Beads of sweat lined his brow. After attaching the sticky pads to the dog's head and chest, Wily let out a wheezy sigh.

Doc's tall frame loomed over his shoulder. Devon sat on the chair a few feet away. Spider Woman watched from the other end of the gurney, her arms still folded across her chest.

Mindia stood calmly at Wily's side. She patted his hand. "Trust yourself."

"Everyone stand back. This is electricity," Wily said.

Devon scooted his chair back and the legs scraped against the tiled floor.

Doc and Mindia took a step toward the door. Spider Woman didn't budge. She stood at the end of the gurney.

Wily threw the switch on and held his breath.

Nothing happened.

Droplets of sweat trickled down his back.

The room was quiet except for the beeping noise of the machine.

Oh, no. It's not going to work. Think. Wily flicked the switch off and checked the wire connections to the box. One wire was loose. He twisted it around the terminal again and rechecked all the other wires. "One more time."

He flicked the switch again and squeezed his eyes tight. Black snakes wiggled underneath his lids, but slowly they disappeared and one by one, each snake was replaced with a ball of white light. He opened his eyes.

Thor's body began to turn colors—like Sport's had. Thor glowed a golden color, then red, then white.

No one moved. Doc gasped.

Mindia moved closer, her shoulder touching Wily's.

Thor's vital monitor beeped louder and quicker and then faded to its original humming. His chest pulsed from his quickened breaths. His eyes blinked open, and he lifted his head toward Wily.

Mindia jumped. "You did it."

Doc unstrapped Thor's facemask. "He sure did."

Wily beamed. He'd done it. He'd really saved the dog.

Mindia held her hand in the air. "Wait. Thor says, '*Thanks, kid. How did you do that?*'"

The dog's mouth moved like he was actually forming words.

Wily shrieked and jumped back, knocking over an IV pole. It clanked onto the tile and almost tipped Mindia off her feet. The dog's queer expression reminded Wily of an animal horror show.

The dog snickered at Wily's reaction and lifted his head off the gurney.

"Thor says, '*It's not every day you see a beast like me speak, is it? Can you unstrap me from that electricity before I blow up?*'" Mindia continued to speak for Thor.

"Oh, sure." Wily drew closer and flipped the switch off, shaking his head in disbelief. He was communicating with a dog.

The dog sat up on the table and licked his chops.

Mindia interpreted again, "*Doc, will you help me down?*"

Doc carefully lifted Thor onto the floor.

Thor faced Wily.

Wily's mouth still hung open. He closed it.

The dog put his right paw up as though he wanted to high-five Wily.

"*You saved my life. I'm forever in your debt,*" Mindia said for the dog.

Wily lifted his hand and gently touched the dog's paw. "No problem." He couldn't believe he was giving a dog a high-five. Weird. Very weird.

Spider Woman clopped out of the room, her hooves click-clacking on the floor.

"What's wrong with her?" Wily asked.

"Don't pay her any attention," Doc said.

Wily wasn't so sure. "Now what?"

Doc put his arm around Wily. "What you did will never be forgotten. It will go into the history of the canine race." He turned to Mindia. "Make sure to put this event in the record book and give it today's date." Then he called to Thor. "Follow me, we'll go to the computer room."

Computer room? "Do I get to go, too?" Wily asked.

Mindia exchanged glances with the others in the room.

Doc clamped a hand on Wily's shoulder. "Of course. You're officially one of us now, a part of the team."

Wily stood a little taller, but his throat went dry. Being a part of their team sounded both exciting and frightening.

As they turned to go to the computer room, the door swung open.

A bearded centaur, wearing overalls over his two front legs and suspenders across his hairy chest, clippety-clopped awkwardly through the doorway. A gold medallion dangled from his neck.

CHAPTER NINE

The centaur's face was that of a human, with gray hair and a beard that bristled down his hard-angled jaw. Wide yellow-stained teeth flashed a snide smile. He had four-square hooves and a tail that swooshed at his backside. On his back was a large, slick, green frog with bulging eyes and a protruding, beating throat. The frog wore a pink tutu and a gold crown on her head.

Wily shrunk back from the strange creatures, then shut his eyes as he had with the spidery centauride, hoping the vision would go away. But when he opened them, the same horse, er, man, stood in the same place with the same frog on his back. Wily squirmed out a smile as he took in the centaur's appearance and fought an internal battle to hold his expression in neutral. No good could come from offending the beast.

The tension in the room thickened.

The horse-man clapped. "Well done." He clip-clopped toward Wily with the frog gripping his back. "Welcome to the team." He hiked his palm out for Wily to shake. "Call me DH." His gruff voice snarled as he glared through brown eyes that seemed to darken by the moment, blackening to the color of soot.

Wily debated whether to give him his hand or not. Did the DH want to shake or was this a joke? Wily extended his palm, deciding it would be better to believe the DH had positive intentions. "Nice to meet you, er, sir."

The DH dropped his hand without taking Wily's, giving him a grin instead.

Wily let his hand drop and took two steps back.

"What? Are you afraid of me?" DH laughed, a deep throaty sound, his breath emitting the combined scent of grass and decaying teeth.

"Er, it's just … that … I …"

"—never saw a man like me before?" His gaze flicked toward Doc. "I'm surprised the good ole Doc here didn't give you a full-blown description of me by now."

Doc zipped his jacket up and down, seemingly nervous.

"Well then, let me explain who I am." DH linked eyes with Wily. "I'm the Dark Horse from the Chiron tribe, the oldest and wisest of the centaurs. I'm an immortal. Do you know what that means?"

"You can't die," Wily said.

"That's right." He grinned, showing the stained teeth in his mouth cave, but Wily doubted this centaur's smile was genuine.

The horse paced the room, the frog tilting its head at Wily. "I'm the ancient trainer of heroes, and I've been running this ship for over a hundred years, training kids like you, using their talents to expose the people on earth who destroyed my race many years ago and those who intend to destroy it again." He stopped in front of Wily. "You see, if all the dogs die, my race will never return. I can't let that happen. You understand, don't you?"

Wily nodded, even though he didn't understand.

"The girl on my back is Orbita." He stroked the frog with his finger. "Isn't she beautiful?"

Wily's eyes shifted to the frog that seemed to give a smug smile. There was nothing beautiful about her. She looked as slimy and web-footed as all the other frogs he'd splayed in his kitchen. But he wouldn't dare disagree. He had a feeling that she meant more to the DH than anyone in the room.

Wily waved to her. "Yes, she's … charming. Hi."

The centaur crossed to Thor. "Glad to see you well again." He nodded to Wily. "Your skills will come in handy, but now you're stuck here with the rest of us. You know that, right?"

Wily nodded. DH was close enough that Wily smelled his breath again and thought he'd gag.

The DH laughed a high-pitched squeal like a horse's neigh.

But nothing seemed funny.

"Let me explain what I do here so there's no misunderstanding." He paused, his eyes shifting to Mindia, Devon, Doc, and Thor before resting on Wily. "I run this ship, give the orders, and train my staff. You work for me now. And since you're a part of this team you're here until you're twenty-one. At that point we'll strip your memory and plant you back on earth, but you'll never use your powers again or remember any of us. We'll give you a new identity, and you'll be free to live the rest of your life. Does that sound fair to you?"

No, but Wily didn't think it would be safe to voice his opinion.

"No one has ever escaped, although they've tried." He turned sharply to Devon.

Devon stared at the floor.

"Devon can explain the consequences, can't you, son?"

Devon stayed silent.

The DH whirled back to Wily. "It's not that I'm a bad guy. It's just that my race is at stake. I can't take any chances. It would change the whole course of the world … my future … and Orbita's." He glanced at Doc who nodded, as if agreeing.

The centaur's eyes narrowed. He gave Wily a smoldering glare. "But you aren't going to be one of those who try to escape, are you?"

Wily's tongue felt as thick as mud. He couldn't answer because he'd have to lie. He wanted to go home. Now.

The DH hammered his hoof on the floor, the sound ricocheting off the metallic walls as loudly and as forcefully as his message.

"Well?" the DH asked.

Wily jumped. "No, sir."

"I didn't think so." The centaur smiled, his wiry beard rising with his lips. "Doc, give him the chip to swallow. I can't be too careful." He raised his hand to cradle the medallion around his neck.

"The chip?"

Doc nodded. "It's a way to track you. The chip will imbed in the lining of your gut. It can triangulate your position using satellite signals. From the time you swallow the chip, the DH will be able to see where you are on a map. It's electronically connected to his medallion."

Doc nodded toward the medallion that the DH still held, then went to a cabinet, opened a drawer, and pulled out a little ball the size of a Cheerios morsel. He handed it to Wily.

Wily stared at the round object in his sweaty palm.

"Go ahead. Swallow it," the DH ordered.

Mindia, Doc, and Devon stared.

Wily lifted it to his mouth, placed it on his tongue, and considered storing it in his cheek like a squirrel with a nut.

"Don't get cute," the DH said. "Swallow it."

Wily swished it in his mouth with his saliva. He could never swallow pills. His mom gave him the chewable kind. "Can I have a drink of water to help it go down?"

"Give the boy a glass of water," the DH said to Doc.

Doc went to the sink, filled a paper cup with water, and handed it to Wily.

Wily swallowed the water and washed the chip down his throat. He coughed and handed the empty cup to Doc.

"Open your mouth." The DH took a step toward Wily and peered inside. "Lift your tongue."

Wily did as he was ordered to do.

"Okay then." The DH lifted the medallion and slid a tiny lever on the front to the right. "Perfect." He stepped to the door with a flourish and yanked the handle to go. "Carry on. Find a way to nail the creeps who are behind this plague, and stop them soon."

Orbita blinked her bulging eyes and croaked just before the door creaked closed.

As soon as they were gone, Doc exhaled loudly.

Mindia tapped Wily on the shoulder and put her finger to her lips, silencing Wily's unspoken thoughts, which were: *what had he done, what was he going to do next, and why was the centaur so fond of Orbita?*

Even though DH seemed to want to do the right thing by saving the dogs, something felt wrong. What was his real motivation?

Mindia mouthed but didn't speak, "We'll explain everything later. He's probably listening."

Wily nodded. They all stared at one another and sighed. Even though DH had left the room, his presence and his stench still lingered.

Thor sat on the floor next to Doc, his tongue drooping, his head hanging low. "*I could use some grub and water to line my raw throat. Let's go to the cafeteria,*" Mindia said for him.

"Great idea," Devon said. "Let's get him something to eat and then get to work. We'll have to hurry."

"Take it easy, Thor. You're still recovering from the wound," Doc said.

Wily was hungry, but still numb from the entire morning—his abduction, the DH, and the shock that his invention had worked. Twice. "Will my box be safe in here?"

"Maybe not," Devon said, moving toward the contraption. "To be sure, let's lock it in the closet."

After Wily gathered the rest of the supplies, Devon placed them with the box and locked the closet. Wily glanced at his pajamas. "You … wouldn't happen to have a change of clothes for me, do you?"

Devon snickered. "We'll take you to the laundry center. You should be able to find a new jersey and a pair of sweats." He turned to Mindia and Doc. "Go ahead to the cafeteria. We'll meet you in there in a few minutes."

CHAPTER TEN

After Wily and Devon made a stop in the laundry room, and Wily dressed in sweats and a baggy T-shirt, Devon escorted him to the kitchen.

A middle-aged woman wearing a large pink bow in her hair and a pink apron around her waist with *The Perfect Chef* printed across the front, stood behind a grill, cutting vegetables that Wily had never seen before—plump purple and orange items as large as tomatoes and green peppers, but freckled with bumps—alien veggies. The woman chopped them at hyper speed. The room smelled beefy, but sweet—like hotdogs on a grill and Juicy Fruit gum—a strange combo, as though the flavors were all wrong.

The chef was nothing like Wily's mother. His mother never wore bows in her hair. He thought of her now and wondered what she was doing. Did she know he was missing yet or was she still sleeping? How long had he been gone? Since there wasn't a clock in sight, he had no idea, but according to his growling stomach, it was at least lunchtime.

Five long tables in an adjacent dining room were occupied with kids Wily hadn't met. They spoke to each other in low monotone voices. No one smiled or laughed.

Mindia, who'd been standing next to the chef, walked over to Wily. "Let me introduce you to Nora."

The cook paused.

"Nora," Mindia said, "this is Wily."

"I see you like to eat." Nora nodded at Wily's pudgy middle.

Wily's face flushed. Great. Just what he needed. Someone else to make fun of his weight.

Nora waved. "Don't worry about it. You'll lose it soon enough around here. My food doesn't make people fat, only full and satisfied."

Doc, who'd finished eating already, held his empty plate in his hand and patted his belly. "I can vouch for that." He set his dirty plate in the sink and stood beside Nora.

Mindia, who was helping Chef Nora pour drinks for the other kids, motioned for Wily to turn around and face the center of the room. "Hey, everyone. This is Wily, our latest crew member. He saved Thor's life."

The room filled with applause and Thor, who was standing beside Wily, barked.

Some of the kids welcomed Wily, but he thought he saw pity in their eyes. He forced himself to smile, basking in the warm feeling of heroism and trying not to think about how trapped he felt. "Does everyone here have … skills?" he asked Mindia.

"Yep and we all work together." She handed him an empty plate, a fork, and a knife.

Wily's pulse skipped at the idea of working together. No one had ever wanted to work with him, or let him be on their team, at least, not in gym class.

Mindia leaned toward Wily's ear. "The kids here aren't like that."

His face grew warm, but before he could say more, Nora cleared her throat to get his attention.

She explained the combo of ingredients, none of which Wily had heard of, nor could he repeat. She tossed the steaming, funny-looking stuff in the skillet, and scooped a spoonful onto Wily's plate, and then Devon's plate.

Thor barked, and Nora spooned another helping onto a clean plate, then placed it on the floor in front of the dog. "Eat up, boy." The dog didn't waste any time lapping it up.

The smell, unlike any scent Wily had sniffed before, wafted up from his plate. He inhaled. The aroma had changed. This reminded him of the rain on a warm day, the sweet sun, and musky earth all rolled together, not something he'd ordinarily think of eating. He shuddered.

Mindia joined Devon and Wily at a nearby table.

Wily took a large bite and instantly wished he hadn't. He gagged at the grainy texture and earthy flavor and spit out his mouthful. He'd never eaten worms before, but he had a feeling this was how they tasted.

Chef Nora, who watched from the stove, laughed.

What was so funny? He was doomed. If he had to stay here forever and eat this food he'd never survive.

Mindia patted his back. "You'll get used to it. We all did, and we love it now."

"You lied to me," Wily stared at her with his mouth agape.

Mindia shook her head. "No, I didn't. You'll get past missing what you used to eat and wonder how you ever liked sweets, salty things, and junk food. But it takes time."

Wily stared at his plate, shrinking from taking another bite. "How much time?"

Mindia shrugged. "It varies with every person."

"Give me a rough estimate."

"About two weeks."

Wily frowned. Two weeks was a long time. He pinched his nose and shoveled the food into his mouth, pausing to gag several times. He was going to miss his mother's meals. Funny that he'd never thought they were any big deal before.

After Wily ate the last bite, Mindia stood up. "We need to get to the computer room. Doc's probably already there."

Devon, still sitting across from Wily, nodded and together they rose, dropped their dirty plates off to Nora, and followed Mindia out of the cafeteria and down the hallway. The other kids had gone their separate ways, some leaving together.

Thor meandered gingerly behind Devon, taking careful steps and wincing.

In the gray hallway, Wily walked tentatively, afraid of the shadows. Was the Dark Horse lurking nearby? Would he jump out from a corner or a closed door?

No one was in sight.

They walked in silence, passing the med room where Wily had helped Thor and met the DH. They passed several other closed doors until they got to the one at the end of the hallway. Devon opened the door and ushered them in.

Computers and other rectangular machines whirred and beeped. Green, red, and yellow lights blinked from a control panel. The room's large dome appearance resembled a library on one side and a live theatre with a stage and a black curtain at the other side. One tall and one short microphone stood center stage. Doc waved them over where he sat at a computer desk that faced the stage.

Wily, Devon, and Thor pulled up chairs and gathered around Doc.

Mindia pressed a few buttons at the computer in front of her and loud music played. She put her fingers to her lips and spoke with a low voice close to Wily's ear. "DH listens in on our conversations sometimes so be careful what you say. Here's a bit of history: Orbita used to be a princess hundreds of years ago, until she was turned into a frog."

Orbita, a princess? Not possible.

Mindia continued. "DH fell in love with her but she wouldn't return his affection. She was from a tribe of centaurs who were emotionless. DH's friend, Cressida, convinced DH that she had the potion and the spell to make Orbita fall in love with him, to fill her with compassion and the emotion to love him. But she was jealous of the princess. Cressida loved the DH and wanted him to herself.

"DH was naive about Cressida. He trusted her. It's hard to believe, but one time the DH was tender, trusting those he shouldn't have. Cressida wanted DH to love her instead, but her spell backfired. The centaurs turned to dogs and Orbita turned into a frog.

"Can't the spell be undone?" Wily asked.

Mindia shook her head. "They must wait until 2050 when Orbita will turn to a centauride again and all the dogs will become centaurs or centaurides."

This was so bizarre.

"The DH uses us as his *people*." Mindia continued, "All his compassion is gone. He doesn't trust anyone but Orbita."

"He trusts a frog?"

Mindia nodded. "Seems crazy, doesn't it? And she could care less about him, but he doesn't see that. He's blindly in love with her."

Wily couldn't imagine. He liked frogs, but not as friends. "Frogs don't live that long. What will he do if she dies?"

She shrugged.

"Whatever you do, don't say that in front of him," Devon said.

"When you finally get to leave here," Doc interrupted, "your programmed chip will command you to return in 2050 to fight for his kind. You'll be one of his puppets."

Wily sucked air. If only he could stop this whole nightmare and save the centaurs too. "What about you?" he asked Doc. "You and

Spider Woman are older. Have you been here for a long time?"

"Spider Woman?" Doc asked.

Wily cleared his throat. "Er, the lady centauride with the willowy black dress and long fingernails."

"Oh, you mean Cressida?" Mindia giggled. "I like the name Spider Woman better."

"You mean, *she's* the one who was in love with the DH? She's the one who cast the spell?" Wily asked.

Mindia nodded toward Doc as if she needed permission to answer Wily's question.

Doc leaned toward Wily. "Yes, she was the woman in love with the DH, the one who loathes Orbita."

"Is she still in love with him?"

Mindia chuckled and shrugged. "We're not sure. She doesn't show it. She's supposed to be working on a way to reverse her spell, to make Orbita a centaur again, but we think she has another agenda. For some reason she doesn't seem to care if all the dogs die. That doesn't make sense—not if she wants the rest of her race to return."

This was getting weirder by the moment.

"The DH captured me when I was doing research," Doc said. "I'm a scientist. Apparently I got a little too close to understanding the spell and finding him, so he banned me to this ship. I've lived here for over eighty years now."

Wily squinted at the doctor. "You don't look any older than my parents who are in their forties."

Doc smiled. "Thanks, but I'm 120 years old."

Mindia continued. "People don't age on this ship. The atmosphere keeps them locked in the present even though time on the outside of the ship ticks away. We only age when we leave here—which isn't often."

Wily shook his head. "You mean I'm going to stay eleven years old forever?"

She nodded. "You'll stay the same age you are now as long as you're here. But when you leave here you'll age in the usual progression."

"How old are you?" Wily waited for her answer.

Tears filled her eyes, but she looked away and when she turned back there was no sign of sadness. "I'm twenty-one."

Wily gasped. "You don't look a day over thirteen."

"That's how old I was when I first arrived."

"If you're twenty-one. then do you get to go home soon?" Wily asked.

"He makes certain kids stay longer. He needs my mind," she said.

Devon crossed his arms and set his jaw. "Even though he says we can choose when we're twenty-one to leave, some of us aren't given a choice."

"Why can't you use your mind on him?" Wily said to Mindia. "Can't you make him do something that will help?"

Mindia shook her head. "It doesn't work on him. He's not human."

Wily had never felt so scared. There had to be a way out of there. He glanced at Devon. What had he done to attempt an escape? The sooner he learned how, the better.

Mindia touched his arm. "Be careful."

Wily was certain she'd read his mind. "Where will my parents think I've gone?"

Doc squeezed Wily's shoulder. "They'll think you vanished. The police will issue an Amber Alert, but there's no way to explain this to them. The police will come, search the property near your home, and your photo will be placed on every telephone pole and bulletin board across the US, but they won't find you, not even a trace as to where you have gone." His voice was solemn.

Wily choked back tears. He would not cry in front of these people. They were all in the same boat. He thought of all the missing children photos on Walmart's bulletin board. His photo would be there soon. He wished he could see his parents and tell them he was okay.

The music stopped, apparently at the end of the song, and the room went silent.

CHAPTER ELEVEN

Wily couldn't stop thinking of his parents. What were they doing now? Where would they look for him? He wanted to see them again, but this mission had only begun. He had to focus on saving the dogs first, and then he'd worry about getting home again.

Devon, Mindia, and Doc exchanged glances. They still sat in a circle in the computer room. The music had stopped a minute ago, but no one said a word, no one moved.

Doc cleared his throat. "We need to debrief Thor and videotape him. Time is of the essence." He opened a drawer and pulled out earphones.

The Great Dane, who had been dozing on the floor next to Doc's feet, pulled himself to all fours and sat while Doc adjusted the earphones to his head. Then he strolled up the stairs and onto the mini stage in front of the camera.

Devon tended the camera equipment, clicking buttons and squinting over a keyboard. "All set," he said. A red light above the camera flickered.

Wily rolled his chair between Mindia and Doc, watching, listening, and observing.

"Thor, start at the beginning," Doc said. "Who's behind this, and what did you find out?"

The dog's tongue flopped out of his mouth, and he cocked his head as if figuring out where to begin. Words on the monitor in front of Devon appeared.

"There's a leak somewhere on this ship. It's the only explanation."

Wow. They could see the dog's thoughts? How was this possible? It was amazing.

"A leak?" Mindia said.

Devon gasped.

Thor nodded. *"They knew I was coming. They were prepared for me."*

"How could they have known?" Doc asked. "No one knew you were going but us." He scratched his chin and scanned everyone in the room, suspiciously.

Wily threw up a hand. "Don't look at me. I just got here."

Doc nodded to Thor. "Go ahead."

"It's a miracle I got out."

Wily wanted to giggle about them communicating with a dog. If he could learn how to do this, he could talk to Sport. Sport? Was he still alive?

"The production line is at the abandoned Justin Mill Factory," the dog said.

The Justin Mill Factory? That was two blocks from Wily's school.

The dog's gaze shifted toward Wily. *"And it's a miracle I'm alive now, thanks to you."*

Wily smiled, but maybe he should have failed. Maybe then he'd be home now.

No, he'd done the right thing. He had to save the dogs and now there was no going back. It was better not to think about what might have happened if he'd failed. He hadn't. He'd saved Thor, which might save the canine race. He had to keep going.

Thor continued. *"The man behind it all is no other than Mortimer Lassiter."*

This time Doc slapped his leg. "I'll be doggone."

"Who's he?" Wily said.

Devon swiveled in his chair and clicked the keyboard. "Let me retrieve his bio on the screen." The screen's image switched to a photo of a middle-aged man with gray hair, glasses, and a white-toothed smile.

He reminded Wily of a politician in his town—perfect tie, blue suit, charisma. Wily had seen him before, but where? On TV?

Doc crossed his arms over his chest and rested his finger on his chin. "He's the chief executive officer for the largest pharmaceutical company worldwide, Helms & Johnson. You've probably seen him on television because of the dog crisis. He makes it sound like his company is working to find a cure, doing everything they can to find the answers." Doc clucked his tongue.

Thor growled and the screen switched back to his thoughts. *"He's doing everything he can, all right, everything he can to kill the canine race."* He paced in front of them. *"Let me explain. He needs dog cell tissues to make an ingredient that can mend bones in humans. It's harvested and injected into elderly people who are suffering from bone loss, making old bones young again. Once the ingredient is injected into the human, the good cells attack the bad ones and thicken the bones."*

Wily didn't understand. "Why can't they ask dog owners to bring their dogs in to a clinic to extract the cells? Why do they have to kill them first?"

"Good question," Thor said. *"The only way they can get the cells is if the dog swallows a chemical first—which when combined with their ingredient, interrelates to produce the end result drug, the one that will make them billions of dollars. Unfortunately, once the chemical is consumed, it kills the dog. It'll make old people young again, but it'll kill the dog race first."*

"How do they get the dogs to ingest the pill?" Mindia asked.

"They're selling it at health food pet stores as treats," Thor said.

Wily whistled. "Can't they find a way to make it work without killing the dogs?"

Thor shook his head. *"Apparently not."*

Wily's scientific mind reeled. If he knew more about the cells and the enzymes maybe he could find a way. Maybe he could use his knowledge as leverage.

Devon scratched his chin. "But not all dogs eat those treats from the health food stores."

Thor stopped pacing. *"True, but once a dog ingests the treat it infects them like a virus. Then it spreads to other dogs within a five-mile radius—even if they're not ingesting the treat. It's highly contagious."*

"That's insane," Wily said. That's probably how Sport got it—from Pookie across the street.

Devon's brow creased. "But how are they getting the dead dog's bodies to extract the solution?"

Wily knew. He'd seen it happen to Pookie. The man in white in the truck.

"The staff at Helms & Johnson," Thor said, *"are telling the government that the dogs are contaminated and need to be disposed of in a proper fashion or humans will be at risk."*

"That's such a lie," Mindia said in her soft voice. "Certainly there are people in the company who don't believe this."

"The government is in on this too?" Wily asked.

Thor shook his head. *"I doubt it. They only know what they're being told. They think the dogs are contaminated, so of course they're concerned about health hazards. But because their necks are on the line to turn our economy around, to raise money for the deficit, and create more jobs—they love this new product that is making our old people young again. Production will employ thousands of people. So it's possible that some of the people know. Their hands are in the money jar."* He stopped to scratch his ear. *"They don't know dog deaths are a result of the drug. Plus, Mortimer believes animals are beneath humans, so he's justifying that it's okay to do this for the betterment of humans."*

The room grew silent.

Thor told them the story of what he saw in the factory, how the two blue-suited men carried a limp man away, and how he got into the office and memorized the computer info.

Wily listened to Thor's story, his mouth burned when he heard about the incinerator. Mrs. Flannigan had been right. He balled his hands into fists. Poor Pookie. "How do we get these guys? Do we have to fight them?" He hoped not.

Mindia threaded her arm through Wily's again and whispered into his ear. "We're going to come up with a plan right now. Together. You're not alone. Good will conquer evil. You'll see."

She was right. He didn't have to do the rest by himself. But a shadow covered his confidence.

Devon clicked on a computer keyboard and a screen rolled down from the ceiling, rattling on its way. Once the screen was in position, he flipped a switch and a map appeared. He typed in the company name, *Helms & Johnson,* and the city, and Google Earth appeared. The camera zoomed in to where the city was on the map. Hidden Falls was located in the northern part of Indiana, hidden among rows of corn fields, little houses, and cow pastures, and only an hour south of where they were in Indiana.

Wily stared at the screen. He'd been to Hidden Falls. It was close to the sand dunes on Lake Michigan. He'd gone there on his first and only camping trip with his parents. It'd been a fiasco. His mother hated sleeping in a tent and mosquitoes chewed his father to pieces. They ended up in a hotel at two a.m.

"Would you recognize the suited guy in a lineup?" Doc asked Thor.

"Possibly," the dog said.

Mindia fiddled with a few more controls on her computer and displayed more photos on the big screen. "Recognize any of these guys?"

Thor padded closer to the screen, squinting and cocking his head. He held up his paw. *"There he is."*

He pointed to a gray-haired man with a double chin.

Doc clucked his tongue. "Brent Hanger. We've suspected him for a long time, but couldn't prove it. Excellent work, Thor." He patted the dog's back. "Did you get a look at the other guy? The one they knocked off?"

Thor panted. *"No, sorry. I didn't."*

Knocked off? Wily didn't like the sound of that.

CHAPTER TWELVE

Wily waited for someone to say something. His leg twitched. He didn't like the thought of criminals using guns and the possibility of him getting shot. His stomach churned, and it wasn't from hunger. Would they expect him to carry a weapon? He didn't know how to hold a gun, let alone shoot one.

Doc nodded toward the conference table in the middle of the room. "Let's move over there and put together a plan."

"*Hey guys,*" Thor's word appeared on the screen, "*I need to snooze for a few. I'm beat, and if I'm going to jump back in the game, I need to sleep.*"

Wily couldn't blame the guy.

Thor crawled under the conference table, curled into a ball, and fell asleep.

The others moved to the table. Wily followed.

Devon carried a laptop computer with him. After he sat, he clicked a few keys and a hologram, a three-dimensional model of the *Helms & Johnson* building, appeared on the tabletop. "This is how I picture us taking them down."

For the next hour, the team laid out their plan to find the information that would expose the bad guys and stop the dogs from dying.

Wily trembled at carrying out his part. He was far more comfortable taking things apart and interpreting data than traveling in a flying craft and confronting criminals as a spy. He needed to push himself, face his fears.

Devon thumped his fist on the table. "We need everyone's part to be executed properly or the plan will fail. We have to wait until morning after their burglar alarms are deactivated. We can't go tonight. That's too risky." He paused. "Any questions?"

One by one, they shook their heads.

Wily understood what he had to do.

"We'll meet back here at 7:00 a.m. tomorrow. Sharp." Devon stood with his computer in his hands and crossed the room.

Wily didn't move. He tried to focus on what Devon had said about Wily's part, but every nerve jittered in his body. "Doc, you said I could see my parents from up here."

Doc sighed. "I don't recommend it. You might not like what you see, and there's nothing you can do about it. Seeing them will only cause pain." He flashed a look in Mindia's direction.

Mindia shook her head. "Yeah, it's not such a good idea, but I understand why you want to look." Her eyelids drooped sadly.

Wily hesitated at their warning. But he really wanted to see his parents. He wanted to make sure Sport was still alive, see his mother's smile while she cooked, and his father watching baseball game reruns. He wanted to know they were okay. "Yes, I want to see them."

Doc rolled his chair toward a large clear glass globe at the end of his desk and waved for Wily to join him.

Wily had noticed the globe earlier and wondered what it was.

"Pull up a chair," Doc said.

Wily scooted a chair across from Doc, the ball positioned between them.

Mindia and Devon stood quietly behind Wily, watching.

Doc typed on a keyboard near the ball. "Go ahead and place your hands on the side of it."

Wily wiped his sweaty palms on his pants, and then hesitantly set them on the smooth, cold globe.

Doc clicked more keys. "Let me pull up your address."

"You know it?"

Doc glanced over the top of his glasses. "You're in the system, kid. We've been to your house, remember?"

"Oh yeah." He cheeks flamed.

Doc clicked one last key and the ball lit up. Inside, beneath Wily's fingers, was a scene like a snow globe—a real scene with the outside of his house in full view. The yellow daffodils along the sidewalk leading to the front porch were budding, and he smelled a pile of Sport's poop. The trail in the woods leading down to the creek was deserted. The water gurgled in the stream and a huge frog jumped off a rock with a *kerplunk.*

He stopped short, holding his breath, and squinted, expecting Sport to bound out of the side door. But he didn't. There were no cars in the driveway, not a soul around. He glided and weaved along every curve of the property. His heart raced. His fingers turned icy. Were his parents inside?

"I can take you in if you want to go," Doc said.

"Don't do it," Mindia said, placing her hand on Wily's arm.

But Wily couldn't resist. His curiosity far outweighed her warning. He nodded at Doc and his fingers tensed as he stared intently at the globe.

Doc clicked a few more keys and the camera zoomed in through the living room window. Wily hyper focused. The TV was off, but the lights were on.

His mother entered the room from her bedroom. Dark crescent-moon shaped bags glared beneath her red eyes, and she held something in her fist. Sport followed her into the room. Thank goodness he was still alive. The dog paced at her side and ran to his food bowl and back again, but his mother seemed lost in another world. She opened her fist to reveal a wadded tissue and blotted her eyes. She sunk into a chair and pressed the tissue to her temple.

"Mom, feed Sport," Wily shouted at the ball, but of course she couldn't hear him.

The dog ran to his bowl, took it in his jowls, and dropped it in Wily's mother's lap. Her eyes widened and she stroked Sport's head as if seeing him for the first time. She got up, went to the pantry, and fed the dog.

Wily sighed. "I miss your cooking, Mom. Where's Dad?"

Her cell phone on the end table rang. Mrs. Coldren reached for it. "Ben, where are you? Did they find Wily?"

She paused.

"You're at the hospital?" She shot out of her chair. "Are you okay?"

Wily sucked in a breath.

His mother fell back into the chair, her hand on her heart. "Thank goodness. What happened?"

She listened for a few minutes. "I'll be right there." She hung up, ran to the kitchen for her purse, then headed into the garage.

Wily shot out of the chair and his fingers lost contact with the globe. He shouted as the image dimmed. "I need to find out if my dad is okay." His heart pounded in his chest. He needed to get home.

Doc clicked a button on the computer and the ball went black. He patted Wily's arm. "It's better not to look anymore."

Tears stung Wily's eyes. "I have to go."

Devon patted his back. "No, you don't. It sucks, but it's beyond your control."

Wily paced. "I can't give up. My mom needs me."

Devon opened his mouth to say something, but closed it before uttering a word.

Mindia put her finger over her lips and glanced at the door in warning.

Wily stomped his foot. "I don't care if he's listening. I want to go home."

Mindia shook her head again. "He'd harm our families." Her voice was barely audible.

"What?" Wily asked. He'd hurt their families?

The room suddenly went cold.

Devon nodded.

Wily sucked in a ragged breath. A rancid taste filled his mouth. *No. There has to be another way.*

Wily wanted to shout at the top of his lungs. He swallowed hard. It was better to reel in his emotions. He heaved a deep long sigh, and his father's words suddenly popped in his head, *Hit them where they're weak. Wily, in life when you want to win the game, you have to find what the opponent needs and hold it back, use it as leverage or bait.* What was the Dark Horse's weakness?

Orbita.

Mindia cocked her head at his thoughts. "Be careful."

Wily thought harder. He had to make his expertise something the DH couldn't live without and use it as leverage. What if he came up with a way to resurrect all the dead dogs, bring them back to life? The DH would have more centaurs in 2050. But Wily would need to build his box to work on more than one dog at a time. He'd need more supplies, batteries, electronic terminal boxes.

Mindia, who still stood beside Wily, nodded her head, raising her finger to her lips. "We have the things you need."

"Really?"

She nodded again. "I'm sorry for invading your thoughts again. For some reason they sound louder than the others in the room. I know I told you I wouldn't read your mind, but I can't seem to stop."

Weird girl. Shoot, he smacked his forehead with his palm.

She frowned.

"I'm … sorry," he stammered. "I've never met anyone like you. That's all."

"It's okay. I know I'm weird."

"It's a good weird though," Wily said.

"Come, follow me." She waved for him to go with her. "I'll show you the research laboratory."

He hesitated, looking at Devon. "Are we done here?"

Doc and Devon nodded, both apparently absorbed in their own thoughts.

Wily's hope skipped, eager to see the lab. He followed her out of the room.

"The resources we have here are pretty amazing, actually," Mindia said over her shoulder as she led the way out the door and down a different hall.

#

When Mindia opened the door to the science lab, Wily's eyes widened. The square room, which smelled of rubbing alcohol and chemicals, had rows of black tables. Each was equipped with high-powered microscopes, computer monitors, and glass vials—all the equipment he'd need, all the equipment he longed to have in his home. The room was a dream come true. Several glass terrarium-type crates filled with white rats sat on one shelf. A smile creased his face.

Other kids, dressed in lab coats and surgical masks, were bent over scopes and computers. They glanced up at him. Some waved, but most seemed too focused on their work to notice him.

Mindia reached inside a closet and pulled out lab coats and surgical masks. She handed him one of each and they garbed up.

Mindia pointed to various supplies around the room. "Every corner is a different station with a different purpose."

One kid, who wore goggles, stood over an area tagged CAUTION. She pointed to him. "That's the fume cupboard, so if you're going to work on some powerful smelling stuff you might want to use that area."

"Is there an electrical area with a power supply and voltage meters?"

"Sure, over here." She crossed the room to the west corner where a tall thin boy with eye protectors stood over a small motor of some sort. The kid looked up. "Hey."

Mindia spoke first. "Wily, this is our ship's engineer, Bean."

Wily nodded. "Nice to meet you."

"Awesome." The boy set his tools down and flung off his glasses, holding his gloved hand up for a high-five. "I heard you saved Thor's life."

Wily smiled and returned the greeting. He puffed out his chest. "Thanks."

"Bean is familiar with electricity," Mindia said.

"Not like he is, though," Bean said, pointing to Wily. "Playing with voltage is *not* my thing." He let out a long sigh and nodded toward the rats in the cages above his workspace. "And I get woozy just seeing the animals." He peeled off his gloves and threw them in the garbage bin. "Bring on the engines and the cold machines, and I'm in my zone."

After Bean left, Mindia and Wily stood side-by-side at the workstation.

"I don't think you need to study this science," Mindia said. "I think the power is in *you*, it's your *gift*. It's not something you can prove like a theory."

Wily stared at her. Was she crazy? "You think I can wave my hands and resurrect animals? You're wrong. I can't make any of this happen without the proper tools and supplies. It doesn't come from me; the power comes from the source."

"Where do my powers come from then? They can't be explained or proven like science."

"That's true. I don't know how yours work, but they're not normal. They're—"

"—weird, right? Like me?" She dropped her head.

"No. I mean …" Now he'd hurt her feelings. "But what I did with Thor was science."

"If you say so." As she left the room, she said over her shoulder, "I'll be in the computer lab when you're done, if you need anything."

Wily nodded. How could she think he had powers? There was nothing powerful about him, except for his appetite. He shook his head.

The other kids in the room were bent over their tables. Some had earphones plugged in, others were writing notes, and a few were using chemicals and vials. Wily needed to get to work too. He didn't have much time to test his theory.

He scanned the room for supplies. One shelf in the corner was labeled electrical supplies, wires, and batteries. There he found a circuit board, an alternator, resistors, inductors, and transistors. He was going to have to build a duplicate black box only a little different. He hoped he could remember what he'd done at home.

He worked for a solid hour, totally absorbed in every detail. Finally, when he thought he'd duplicated his black box, he observed the rats in various crates. One crate was filled with dead rats, all lying on their sides. He opened the wired top and took three stiffs out and splayed them across a board on the desk in front of him, as he had with his frogs. He put them in a row and connected them with the electrodes. Then he channeled the wires to the power supply.

He paused. The rats were much smaller specimens than a dog. If the current was too strong, he could fry them, or worse yet, cause a fire. Maybe he needed to reduce the electrodes. He took one off.

Yeah, that should do it. He flipped the switch. The rat closest to him twitched, but only for a few seconds, the others didn't move.

Wily turned the power off, then back on. The same rat twitched again, but only for a few seconds.

The voices in the room halted and a shadow hung over his shoulder. The DH stood less than a foot away—observing him. Orbita sat on his back, her thin sucker-like feet clinging to him.

Wily jumped, startling at their proximity.

CHAPTER THIRTEEN

The scent of oats and hay emanated from the DH as he lurked over Wily's shoulder. Wily forced himself to stay calm. *Never let them see you sweat.* His father's words came back to him again. Funny how he'd let them go in one ear and out the other thinking he'd never need them.

"What are you trying to do?" the man-horse asked.

Wily faced him.

Orbita croaked, her bulging eyes piercing Wily.

Keep your voice steady. "I want to see if I can bring multiple rats back to life at the same time."

"Why?"

This was his chance. "Maybe I could save the dogs that have died. People are sad about losing them."

"Why do you care about those people? You don't even know them."

Wily shrugged, afraid to say more, but feeling that he needed to. He wanted to say that the dogs mattered, and that not knowing their owners didn't stop him from feeling sorry for them. But he didn't say anything because suddenly a spark flew from the rat. An odor of burning hair singed Wily's nostrils.

Shoot. In the distraction, he'd forgotten that the voltage was still turned on.

Smoke billowed from the first dead rat. Quickly, Wily reached to turn the power switch off, but his sleeve caught fire.

"Ouch." He flinched and shook his arm. Flames spread up his sleeve. Turning away from the rat, Wily flung his arm and accidentally hit the DH smack in the face, setting his wiry beard on fire.

The DH reared up on his back legs. Panic filled his eyes and widening his nostrils. He let out a screaming shrill neigh. "Put it out. Put it out."

The kids in the room stood frozen, watching. Orbita clung to the DH's back, her mouth open.

Wily rushed to the sink several yards away, turned on the faucet, and ran his arm under the water. He ripped off his shirt and ran it under the water while the DH continued spinning and dancing in circles screaming and patting his hands across his face.

Wily crossed toward him and flung his wet shirt onto the horse's beard and face, pressing the wet rag and smearing it over his mouth and eyes until the flames died.

Once the fire was out, the DH struck Wily across the face, knocking him to the floor. "You stupid boy. Look what you've done." He stormed out of the room, his hooves clopping across the tile floor, Orbita still glued to his back.

The door slammed shut and the room grew noisy.

Wily lay on the floor. The room spun.

Kids cheered. Someone helped Wily up and said, "That was cool."

Cool?

"You should have let him burn," one kid said.

Wily shuddered at the thought of watching anyone burn.

The rat was no longer white, but charred black, smoke still billowing from its body like Wily's hope.

He lifted his hand to his face, feeling the heat rise from the DH's slap. He'd not only failed at resurrecting the rats, he'd injured someone. He could have burned down the craft. He returned to the faucet and let the cool water run over his stinging arm and hand.

The kids in the room stared at him.

"Yeah, you should have let him burn," a girl said.

Another boy patted him on the back. "You okay?"

Wily nodded but wanted to cry. He concealed the lump of disappointment in his throat. He didn't like that they were happy about him burning the DH. It felt wrong.

The door opened and Mindia rushed in. "What happened?" Her voice was soft and calm. "We could hear the DH screaming all the way down the hall."

Wily explained what had happened as the water ran down his arm. His face flushed as he realized he was standing in front of a room full of kids without a shirt on, his belly flab hanging over the top of his pants. Thankfully, Mindia's eyes never left his arm.

She reached for the paper towel, ran it under water, and set it on his arm. "Come with me. I'll put some salve on those burns. Looks like you've got a few blisters already. She led him to the infirmary, where Thor had been when Wily first met him. Once inside, she had him sit on the examining table.

"Let me see."

He held out his hand, feeling strange that a girl was helping him, a girl who was close to his age, but not really.

"Don't worry about your shirt. We'll get you another one," Mindia said. She squinted and turned his arm one way, then the other. She opened drawers and gathered supplies. "You'll need to keep these clean and dry so they don't get infected." She applied a goop to his burns and wrapped a light bandage.

"Will you bandage *him* too? I burned his face."

She paused, linking eyes with him. "He can find his own help." Mindia set the supplies back into the appropriate drawers. "Burning him is the only way to kill him."

Wily shuddered at her icy tone.

If only he could find a way for the DH and the kids to work together. He understood why no one liked the horse, but maybe if Wily taught him how to have compassion, the kids would care for him more.

CHAPTER FOURTEEN

Wily found another new sweatshirt, still wrapped in plastic, in the gym and carefully lifted it over his head, without disturbing the bandages Mindia had applied. He'd told her he'd be in the dining room for dinner shortly, but first there was something he needed to do. He didn't tell her what it was, and he'd kept his plan out of his thoughts so she couldn't read them.

He left the locker room and returned to the infirmary for burn supplies—the ones Mindia had used on him. He gathered them and put them in a bag. Then he roamed the halls, read signs, and stopped to peer inside rooms. Where did the DH hide out? It would have to be a large room, maybe with a view of the outside. Probably it would be at the front or back of the ship. He was closer to the front, so he headed there.

Other kids passed him in the hallway. Most said hello or waved—unlike at school where the kids snickered. It was strange that even though he didn't know any of these kids they all seemed to accept him, to like him. He held his head a little higher. Even though he wanted to go home, he felt better about himself here.

At the end of the hall, there were three doors. As he was going to knock at the first one, it opened. A boy came out and Wily could see the room he had been in was a bathroom.

"Excuse me," Wily said, "but can you tell me which room is the DH's?"

The boy paused and lifted his eyebrows. Then he pointed to the door straight ahead. "No one visits him. But if you're sure you want to risk it, then knock three times fast and four times slow, and he'll open the door. He'll think you're the chef." The boy turned to go, but said over his shoulder, "Don't tell him I told you."

Wily thanked him. Maybe he should turn around and forget the whole idea. No. He had to do this. He gulped the bile rising in his throat, made a fist, and knocked three times fast and four times slow.

Nothing happened.

He was about to knock again when the door slowly opened and Cressida, the spider centauride, appeared, standing in a little foyer.

"What do you want?" she asked, keeping her voice low and looking over her shoulder into the room as if waiting for the DH to appear.

Wily licked his lips. "I'd like to ..." His voice cracked. He cleared his throat. "... talk to the Dark Horse, please."

Lines wrinkled on her forehead. "What makes you think he'll see you?"

"Who is it, Cressida?" The DH's voice thundered from somewhere unseen and deep in the room.

"It's the fire-boy," she said over her shoulder.

"Bring him here."

Cressida shook her head at Wily.

Maybe he should leave now while he still had the chance.

Cressida motioned for him to enter, closed the door, turned the deadbolt and led Wily into a large round room. One wall had the largest window he'd ever seen—with a view of the city a mile below. At least twelve TV screens hung to one side, each one displaying a view of a different part of the ship. One was the computer room, the infirmary, the science lab, and other rooms he hadn't yet seen.

The temperature was at least fifteen degrees cooler than the rest of the ship, and the room smelled of the hay that lay stacked in a corner.

The DH sat in a large chair surrounded by pillows. Orbita was perched on a bright red one closest to the horse. He stroked her back with his fingertips, love and compassion in his eyes.

The DH's affectionate expression startled Wily.

"Don't stand there looking at me. Come here, boy, and tell me what you want, but keep your distance."

Wily inched closer, meeting the DH's eyes, but standing ten feet away.

The horse's beard was gone and in its place was flaming red, shiny skin that spread up his cheek, to his eye, and his forehead, blisters already forming.

"I'm sorry for what happened, sir. I never meant to harm you. I came to make sure you were okay and bring you supplies for your wounds." He held up the bag of bandages and salve.

The Dark Horse tilted his head as if in surprise. "Why do you care about me?"

Wily shrugged. He didn't want to tell him that he felt sorry for him, that he knew how it felt to be different, to have others dislike him. Instead, he said, "The burns can become infected. You need to treat them and cover them with a dressing." He lifted his sleeve to display the bandages Mindia had applied. "Like this."

Cressida lingered nearby, her arms crossed. She guffawed loudly enough that Wily could hear, but he ignored her.

The DH smiled. "How kind of you."

Even though the horse had said the words of thanks, Wily didn't believe the DH meant them. They were laced with sarcasm.

"Are you sucking up to me?"

"No, sir."

"Well, it's not going to help you, so turn around and return to the others to capture the dog murderers."

"Yes, sir." Wily placed the supplies on a table and turned to go, his fingers trembling. But he needed to say one more thing. He must if he ever hoped to see his family again. "Sir, I need to go home to help my parents."

The DH laughed. "You can't leave here. Those are the rules."

Anger spread through Wily like a jolt of electricity. "What happened to your compassion, sir?"

The DH glared at him. "What did you say?"

"You have feelings for Orbita."

"Yeah, so?"

"Who will you turn to when she's not around?" Wily asked.

The DH's jaw twitched and he took a quick step toward Wily, his hands in fists. "What's going to happen to her?"

Wily backstepped. "She can't live forever, and you'll need friends."

"Get out." He pointed to the door.

Wily didn't believe that the horse didn't care. Wily knew the pain that came from having no friends. He'd recognized the way it looked, the drooping of the DH's shoulders, the way he twirled the hairs on his beard when he didn't think anyone was looking, the hesitation when he shouted orders, and the way he pretended to be confident, but held his hands together so no one would notice his fingers jittering.

Cressida took a few steps toward him as if waiting to escort him out.

Wily paused. "I read about Chirons in English class. A Chiron was known to be the wisest of all centaurs. To the Greeks he was a close representation of a saint. He was a father figure to many of God's children. Why do you behave like the devil instead? "

"I said get out." The horse took two giant steps toward Wily, his face so close that Wily could smell his yellowed teeth.

Wily refused to move. "If you let the kids return home and asked them to come back here in 2050 to help you reestablish your kind, maybe they would. But first you have to give them a reason to like you."

The DH slapped Wily's face. "I don't care if they like me."

Wily ignored the sting of his cheek.

The DH laughed, a long throaty sound, but it sounded forced.

Maybe Wily struck a nerve.

"I don't need you to lecture me. Go on and get out of here."

Cressida moved toward Wily from where she sat in the corner of the room.

Wily ignored her and kept his eyes on DH. "What if I could increase how many centaurs return in 2050 by thousands, would you let the kids go home then?"

The horse's eyes widened. "How?"

"I could bring the dead dogs back to life." What was he saying? He'd tried and failed moments ago. What made him think he could be successful?

"You can do this?"

Wily nodded. "I think I can."

"You *think* you can? That doesn't sound too positive."

"I need more practice, but if I can bring one animal back to life, why couldn't I bring multiple ones?"

Orbita hopped off the pillow where she'd been laying and jumped onto the ottoman next to Wily. She rubbed her back against his leg.

The DH noticed Orbita's affection toward Wily. His nostrils flared and his face reddened. "Orbita, get back here."

The frog lowered her eyes and blinked at Wily in a flirting way. In one leap she was in his arms.

Wily cringed but held her in his hands.

In two clip-clops the DH yanked Orbita from Wily.

"Look at the way you love her. How would you feel if she died? If you could no longer see her?" Wily cringed at his boldness, but he couldn't stop the words from tumbling out of his mouth. He was certain the DH had compassion—somewhere inside him.

The horse pounded a hoof on the ground. "She's different."

"How?"

"She's the princess of the centaurs, and when our race returns in 2050 the spell will be broken, and she'll reign at my side."

Cressida laughed.

Orbita fluttered her eyes at Wily again.

The DH set his jaw.

"What will you do when 2050 comes and you have no friends, only robotic followers?" Wily should have stopped, but he couldn't.

The DH stood face-to-face with Wily again, gritting his teeth. He was so close Wily could see his blood-shot eyes and the rage bulging in the vein on his neck.

But he saw fear too.

The DH was scared. Maybe no one had ever stood up to him before. Maybe Wily had unraveled his worse fears.

The DH clenched his yellow teeth. "I am the last of my kind whereas there are millions of you." He shook a finger at Wily as if trying to drive home his point. "And if we don't stop these creeps from killing the dogs, they'll kill my race and they'll never return. Do you understand?" If smoke could come out of the DH's ears it probably would have filled the room.

Wily nodded, trying not to flinch or step back. He understood. The DH was scared of never having a friend, of being alone. "I had no part in what happened years ago, sir. I hadn't even been born yet." He lowered his voice a notch. "Maybe you should blame the person responsible for casting a spell in the first place."

Cressida chuckled again. She was sitting at a table, her back to them, putting together a puzzle.

The horse stared hard at her back and then at Wily, his eyes blacker than a moment ago, but there was guilt in his look too. He pointed to the door. "Get out of here before I throw you out."

Wily turned to go, realizing he'd been right. The horse had probably started the whole curse. He was the one responsible for casting the spell.

"Out, I said."

Cressida rose and grabbed Wily's arm and ushered him out.

When the door closed and Wily heard the deadbolt lock, he exhaled. He could have died in there. But he hadn't. And somehow maybe he'd made progress. Even though he'd been thrown out, the DH was rattled.

As he hurried to the dining room to meet the others, he sighed. Maybe he was an idiot for ticking off the DH, but he got the feeling that maybe something he'd said would change the old horse.

CHAPTER FIFTEEN

When Wily walked into the dining room, Doc, Devon, and Mindia were gathered around. Their shoulders slumped. Each person had dark circles under their eyes. Doc yawned.

Wily said hello to Nora who handed him a plate and a scoop of pink and blue food. *This can't be good.* The room smelled like salted peanuts, the kind in the shell he loved to crack open. His appetite raged, but he had a feeling he was going to be disappointed in the food. Oh, what he wouldn't do for a Three Musketeer's bar.

He sat across from Doc and Devon, next to Mindia, all who had started eating.

Doc nodded to Wily, his fork in his hand. "You set him on fire? You could have killed him." He didn't look up, but took a bite of his food.

"I'm sorry. It was an accident," Wily said.

Doc wiped a pink morsel of food from his chin. "Fire is the only thing that *can* kill him." His voice was low enough that those sitting at other tables probably couldn't hear him.

Devon shook his head and scowled, then slammed his fist on the table.

Wily jumped.

Kids from a nearby table looked over at them.

"You had the chance to free us all," Devon said, "but you didn't, you moron."

Moron? Wily hung his head and shrank at Devon's venomous

eyes and the accusatory looks from the others. His face heated. In a few hours, they'd forgotten that he'd saved Thor's life. He recognized their look of disgust and disappointment. The reason he had no friends.

"Promise the next time you get the chance you'll finish him off," Devon said.

Wily sat motionless. He couldn't promise that. But he felt if he didn't the others would hate him forever.

Devon's eyes were locked on Wily's, waiting for an answer. "You can't do it, can you?" He shook his head. "Do you think it's fair that Mindia has been locked here for eight years, that her father is dead and her mother all alone?"

Wily turned to Mindia. "No, it's not fair. I'm sorry."

Mindia cast her eyes downward.

But killing the DH wasn't right either.

"Do you think it's fair that you'll never see *your* family again?" Devon continued.

Wily shook his head. Of course it wasn't fair. "There has to be another way." He voice was barely audible. "I want to find a way."

"You don't think we've tried? I've been stuck here for so long that my family has all died." Spit flew from Devon's mouth.

"I'm sorry." But Wily's apology didn't sound adequate, and he couldn't promise that he would let the DH burn alive if given another opportunity.

They scowled at him. All except Mindia.

She placed her hand on his. "Next time you'll finish him off, won't you?"

He stared at his plate and sensed Mindia's gaze as she waited for an answer.

"I ... I ... I'm not ... sure." He wasn't capable of killing anyone. He looked up.

A tear fell down Mindia's cheek and she turned away.

Wily stared at his food, his appetite gone.

Devon shook his head. "In time you'll think differently." He shoveled in a large spoonful of food. "You all know what to do, tomorrow, right?"

They all nodded.

"Don't forget, if you deviate from the plan, you put others in danger." Devon's brow creased when he looked at Wily.

Wily's face heated. The thought of his mission, high-powered crooks, and loaded guns flushed him into a sweat. He'd do the best he could. That's all he could do.

"Wily, you stay with Mindia," Devon said.

It didn't sound like Devon trusted him.

Thor, who'd been eating nearby, bounded over and sat next to Wily. He yawned and nodded to Mindia.

"He wants to tell you something," Mindia said. "*Look kid, I owe you for saving my life. I'm sorry you're getting the cold shoulder from everyone. They'll come around. It isn't your fault the DH is such a jerk.*"

"Thanks."

"*But if you get another chance, take it.*" He turned to go, his tail wagging as he went.

Even the dog agreed with the others. Wily felt dizzy. He couldn't imagine burning someone alive. He hoped he wouldn't have to, that somehow he'd find another way to free them from the DH's selfish clutches.

#

That night, while everyone slept, Wily couldn't. There was something he had to try. One more time.

He tiptoed down the dimly lit hallway to the infirmary, opened the door and flicked on the light. He crossed the room to the closet to retrieve his black box, but remembered that the door was locked. *What happened to my Swiss Army knife?* He reached into his pocket. *Yes.* It was still there. He'd transferred it after he'd found new clothes in the ship's laundry room. He took the knife, moved to the doorknob, and flipped open the awl blade. Positioning the point inside the lock, he jiggled the knife. The lock released. He opened the door, grabbed the box and the wires, and quickly left the room.

The hallways were deserted. He moved swiftly but quietly.

When he reached the lab, he flicked on one dim light near the table where he'd worked before—where he'd set the DH on fire. He placed the box and supplies at the same table. Thankfully, all his supplies were still there, and someone had removed the charred rat. He plugged the box into the wall outlet.

Sitting in a crate on the shelf above him were four dead white rats, and one that was still alive. He opened the wire lid and took the closest two dead ones in his palm. They were cold and stiff.

He set them on the table in front of him. Sweat formed on his brow. This time he found thin-wired electrodes. They might be more appropriate for a smaller creature. After he rigged the wires onto the rats and connected them to his box, he closed his eyes and flipped the switch.

Slowly, the rats began to glow. First one, then the other. Their white fur turned pink. Their eyes blinked open, then closed again in a twitch. Then their front feet wiggled as if running in a dream.

Wily stifled a gasp and waited. The rats' eyes opened again and locked onto Wily's. Their hair stood on end and high-pitched *weeps* escaped from their mouths. Finally, the rodents stood and scurried away. They ran too fast for Wily to catch them, darting across the lab table and leaping onto another table.

Wily stood stunned, his mouth gaped open. *People from everywhere will want me to bring their loved-ones back to life. This could change the world if it worked on humans.*

He let this idea process for a minute. *It doesn't work with people. Only animals.* He tried to convince himself that it wouldn't work on humans, but a gnawing fear crept into his veins. What if it could?

He must never give anyone the idea that that might be possible.

He hurried back to his room to sleep before their battle tomorrow. He needed a clear head, but he had no idea how he would possibly sleep.

#

The next morning at seven o'clock, Wily, Mindia, Devon, Doc, and Thor walked single-file down the long corridor toward the shuttle. Nora stopped them in the hallway, just outside the cafeteria, her large, pink bow sitting a little crooked on her head. She held paper sacks in her hand. The sight of Nora made him think of his mother and remember all the times she'd been there for him holding out his packed lunch, his homework, giving him a kiss, and telling him she loved him.

She was way too sappy, especially when she said, "You never know when it's the last time we'll see each other. It's important to always say *I love you* before we part."

But remembering her words now made him miss her. The last thing he wanted to do was cry. *Get a grip.*

Mindia walked beside him. "I wish I could say it gets easier, but it doesn't. Some days are better than others though."

Her words speared him in the heart. Bluntly. He was heading out into the world, into who-knew-what storm, and he wouldn't get the chance to tell his mom that he loved her. He thought of his father and tried to remember the last time he'd heard him say those words. Wily couldn't remember the last time he'd said those words to his dad—or if he'd ever said them.

Wily took the bag from Nora and forced a smile.

"You all come back soon and in one piece, you hear?" she said.

"Thanks, Nora," Mindia said. "The food will come in handy."

"Yes, thanks," Wily squeaked, emotion hijacking his voice. He let the others walk ahead of him and stole a peek into the sack. Inside was a plastic bag that looked like it was filled with worms and dirt. He reached in, opened the plastic baggie, and sniffed. He almost gagged. He breathed in through his mouth instead of his nose and pinched the worms between his fingers. Then he threw the contents into his mouth. The food crunched between his teeth, not like a potato chip crunch, but more like a dirty sand crunch that you get after spending the day at the beach.

The bitterness of the aftertaste made him shudder. He closed the bag, certain that he'd get sick if he ate any more. Plus, knowing where he was going and what he would be doing made him more nauseated.

As they approached the craft entrance, no one spoke. This was Wily's chance to be a team player, but no one wanted him on their team—just like at school.

CHAPTER SIXTEEN

Doc, Devon, Mindia, Thor, and Wily, in that order, approached the end of the hall that led to the glass craft. Devon pressed the button and the door hissed as it opened. Wily felt someone standing behind him. He turned. The DH stood two feet away with bandages on his face and Orbita on his back.

"You know what you're supposed to do," the DH said, his eyes skating over each one of them. "I'll be watching. One wrong move …"

And what? What would he do? The others didn't speak or turn to address the horse, and their expressions remained stoic.

Before taking a step into the craft, Wily reached a finger out and stroked Orbita's back.

She closed her eyes and leaned into his finger.

The DH scowled.

Devon climbed up and into the pilot seat at the controls with Doc beside him—pilot and co-pilot. Mindia sat next to Wily in the seats behind the pilots. Thor jumped onto a bench, sighed, and sprawled across it with his head between his paws.

Wily wished he could feel as relaxed as Thor looked. He wanted to tell the others that he was scared, that he didn't think he could carry out their plan, but he didn't. He had a job to do like they did. If he hoped to win their friendship, then he'd have to do his part. His stomach rumbled. The snack twitched and lurched in his gut, its gritty taste still on his tongue.

Doc clicked, pulled, and spun the controls in front of him. Low murmurs between Doc and Devon were undecipherable. When the craft lifted out of the large ship and floated above, Wily's stomach plummeted. He might puke.

"Remember to look straight ahead. Don't look down or to the sides," Mindia said. "If you have to, close your eyes. It helps. I promise, you'll get used to it."

He wasn't so sure he'd ever get used to it. Nor did he want to. He'd only flown once on an airplane and hated it. He'd spilled his guts into a barf bag, and just in time.

For the next half an hour, Wily thought of Sport, his parents, his home, and the kids at school. He'd only been gone for a little more than a day, yet if felt like forever. He'd laid in bed last night unable to sleep, the bed strange and uncomfortable, his thoughts like thunder in a storm, bouncing out of control.

At first he was excited about bringing two lives back from the dead, but then today's duties threaded through those happy thoughts and covered them with dread.

The craft hovered then clunked, jolting him in his seat.

Devon parked the craft in a narrow alley downtown in Hidden Falls, next to the *Helms & Johnson* tower, their target destination, the one with the creeps with guns, and the computer mainframe. The narrow alley was dark because the rising sun was on the other side of the building. Dented garbage bins lined one brick wall, the side they needed to exit.

Wily's fingers trembled as he clipped the leash onto Thor's collar. "You ready?"

Thor nodded.

Wily rubbed the dog's ears, his palms sweaty. Fear clutched a hold on him, like his father's large hand on his shoulder.

Devon placed a curly-haired wig on his head and a Michigan State baseball cap over it. Then he threw on a maintenance shirt and buttoned all but the last button. The front had the words "O's Computers and Maintenance" embroidered on the right side. He opened his wallet and observed his fake ID. "Looks good, Doc."

"Thanks," Doc said.

Devon nodded to them. "We'll meet back here in one hour, if you're not back by that time the ship leaves." He pointed to Doc. "Don't wait for anyone. Not even me."

"Okay." Doc opened a drawer, pulling out three watches. He handed Wily and Mindia one and strapped the last one onto his arm. "Set your watches. The button is on the side here," he demonstrated. "It'll work as a two-way radio if you depress it. Only use it if it's an emergency. Don't draw attention to yourself unless it's absolutely necessary."

Yes, that was part of surviving. When all else failed, create a diversion.

Wily fastened the watch around his wrist and clicked the notch. The speaker over the control desk crinkled with static. Perfect. It worked.

"The alarm will vibrate at precisely 10:00 a.m.," Devon said. "Our goal is to get the evidence and deliver it to the authorities. If you're not here we'll leave and circle back to pick you up, but that's not preferred and could jeopardize our safety. The sooner and quicker we can get in and get out, the better."

Wily nodded.

Mindia placed her steady hand on Wily's arm. "This is the reason we're here. Don't be afraid. It's what keeps us going—the fact that we can expose criminals. Saving the dogs will make missing our families worth it." She averted her gaze out the window. "If you picture the moment when we get the evidence and the criminals are arrested, it'll help you stay focused, help drive your nerves into the ground."

Wily nodded, but a bead of sweat trickled down his back. These guys had shot Thor. They could shoot him too. He went over his assignment in his head. Thor had said to trust him, but Wily wasn't comfortable leaving his life in a dog's hands.

Doc waved good-bye as they turned to go. He would stay in the craft and wait for them to return and be ready to go. "You can do this, kids. I believe in you."

At least someone did.

Wily followed Devon and Mindia out of the ship with Thor on a leash beside him. The smell of garbage and car exhaust wafted up from the alley. When he turned back, the craft door hissed shut and blinked invisible.

Fat graffiti in multiple colors decorated the sides of buildings. Cigarette butts gathered in a crack in the sidewalk. Cars honked in the distance, a dog barked, and bile rose in Wily's mouth.

"Hey, how did you appear out of thin air?" A man, who sat on a concrete balcony several floors up, shouted down to them. He blinked. "Poof—and you appeared." His words were slurred and his hair and clothes were disheveled.

Mindia set her gaze upon the man and swirled her eyes. The guy froze without another word and stared at her. After a few seconds, Mindia's eyes returned to normal. "He won't remember a thing."

Wily paused. She could do that to him too. She already had.

"I wouldn't use it on you," Mindia said, "—unless the DH ordered me too, then I wouldn't have a choice."

Wily hoped that wouldn't happen.

Devon walked ahead down the alley, as planned, and onto the sidewalk near the street. He carried a briefcase and pretended he didn't know any of them.

Mindia, Thor and Wily followed Devon to the street side of the building. Cars zoomed and weaved. A driver honked. People hurried down the sidewalk. Someone blew cigarette smoke in Wily's face. Its stale smell reminded Wily of his dad's brother Jerome. Whenever Jerome visited, the whole house reeked of smoke.

A man, dressed in baggy clothes and wearing sunglasses, sat against the building. He held a cardboard sign: *Please help. Blind. Hungry.* A coffee tin rested between his legs. A passerby threw a coin in where it kerplunked. The blind man nodded in the direction of the passerby, but then he turned and seemed to lock eyes on Wily.

Wily was sure the man could see them and knew that they were up to sneaky business. Or Wily was paranoid. Yes. That's probably all it was.

A bellman in a navy uniform stood at the front door of the tall John Hancock building. Devon flashed a badge at him. The man waved for him to enter.

Sweet. Next it was Wily's turn to get in with Thor. There were going to be deterred. No way was the bellman going to let a dog in the place.

Thor winked at Wily. Obviously he had a plan.

A dark sedan pulled in front of the building as they were about to approach the bellman. The uniformed man proceeded to the curbside to open the doors for the passengers in the car, his back turned to the kids. Mindia, Wily, and Thor hurried into the building unseen. Good. They wouldn't have to use Mindia's spiral eyes to get them inside the building, nor would they have to use a diversion tactic.

They entered the shiny tile-floored lobby, finding it deserted except for a set of escalators whirring to the right. Their footsteps echoed off the marble walls. To their left were rows of silver-keyed mailboxes with typed names and a list of companies. "Johnson & Helms" was located on the tenth floor like they thought. Beyond the mailboxes were rows of elevators. Devon must have made it up to the tenth floor already as no one was waiting.

So far, so good.

Mindia paused at the mailboxes briefly reading the names before they hurried to the elevators. "Lucy Feldor," she whispered. She pressed the UP button. Immediately, the motor clicked.

Wily tapped his foot and held his breath. The sound stopped, a bell dinged, and the door opened.

It was empty. Wily exhaled. Thor's tail wagged.

They hurried in and Mindia pressed the button for the tenth floor.

"That was easy," Wily said, his heart skipping.

"There's a lot more to do," Mindia said. "Devon is counting on us. We need to get the vials and protect him."

Wily's stomach fluttered with a million June bugs.

Mindia patted his arm.

Thor lifted his paw onto Wily's knee.

Mindia interpreted for Thor, "He says, *'Let me handle this. You just react.'*"

"Okay," Wily said.

The elevator stopped. The bell dinged, and the door slowly opened.

Standing in front of the opening was Devon and a blue-uniformed guard. The guard had Devon's permit in his hand and was asking him questions. When he saw Wily and Thor, the guard handed Devon his pass. "Carry on." Then he turned to Wily. "You can't bring a dog up here. How did you get through the front bellman?"

Wily couldn't talk. His mouth felt like cotton.

Mindia stepped in front of him and extended her hand to the guard. "We're here to see my Aunt Lucy. This is her dog." She pointed to Thor. "He's not feeling well, and we're babysitting him for her. He has cancer. Is there any way you could let us see my aunt? This might be the last time she sees her dog alive, sir."

The man wrinkled his brow. "Lucy? You mean, Ms. Feldor?"

"Yes, she's my aunt," Mindia said. She nonchalantly jabbed Wily with her elbow.

Wily nodded.

"That's the biggest dog I've ever seen," a young, red-headed receptionist said, her phone's headset resting on top of her head. She sat at a desk ten yards away with a row of phones in front of her. She opened a drawer. "I have a treat here too. The bank always gives me a few extras for my dog." She kissed the air for Thor to come to her side.

He obeyed, pulling Wily with him.

They approached the desk and she tossed the treat in the air.

Thor snapped the morsel in his mouth in one quick swipe and barked.

"Thank you," Mindia said.

Wily still couldn't speak.

The officer leaned against a high counter on the other side of the receptionist's desk, his elbow resting on it. "Is Ms. Feldor in her office?"

The receptionist looked down at her switchboard. "She is, but she's on the phone. I'll let you know as soon as she's available." A call came in on the switchboard, and she answered the call.

People passed by, seemingly lost in their thoughts. Men and women dressed in suits and carrying briefcases hurried into offices. Some people wore blue scrubs—the kind worn in surgery. Maybe they worked in the lab.

Light filtered in through the windows at the end of the hall casting shards of light onto the carpeted floors. A sweet candle burned nearby. It reminded Wily of his mother, her favorite rose scent. Oh, what he wouldn't do to see her right now.

The officer pointed to a few chairs along one wall. "Have a seat there."

Wily took a seat, Thor beside him, but Mindia paused.

"Officer, do you think I could use the ladies' room while we wait? We had a long walk here and well, I would be most appreciative."

What was she doing? This wasn't in the plan. He was going to be alone with the dog and what if Ms. Feldor appeared? What was he supposed to say to her? "We'll go with you," he said to Mindia.

"No," she said. "Wait here."

Wily's ears buzzed. He took his seat again and bit his lower lip.

"Certainly," the security guard said to Mindia, "I can make an exception. I doubt you could do much harm here. The bathroom is down that hall and to your right." He pointed to the opposite hall. The elevator dinged and the door opened. The guard nodded to two men getting off. "Good afternoon, Mr. Hanger, Mr. Jeffries."

Mindia walked off without a backward glance.

Mr. Hanger? He was the guy who'd shot Thor.

Thor growled.

The men continued off the elevator and walked past the officer toward Wily and Thor.

Wily clamped Thor's mouth shut. "Be good," he said under his breath.

Thor broke free of Wily's hand and army-crawled under the chair, whining quietly.

The men shuffled by, seeming not to notice Thor.

Once the men had passed, Wily exhaled. That was a lucky moment.

The receptionist called out over the counter. "It looks like Ms. Feldor is off her phone now."

Wily's stomach plummeted. This was not good. Now what? Mindia. Where are you?

The guard motioned to Wily. "She's down that hall in room 204, third door on the right."

Wily nodded and stood. "Thank you." The blood rushed to his head and his heart thumped in his ears.

Thor crawled out from under the chair and stood at Wily's side.

Should they wait for Mindia or proceed down the hall without her?

Thor nudged his nose into the back of Wily's thigh, motioning for him to walk.

Wily's fingers shook. He hated indecision. Mindia was supposed to do this part. Something must have happened to her.

He'd have to steal the vial without her.

He exhaled and pretended to know what he was doing. Resuming his jaunt down the hall, he took small steps. When he turned the corner toward Ms. Feldor's office, the long corridor appeared—like Devon had showed them on the hologram. The computer room's double doors were at the other end—that's where Devon was supposed to be.

The fire alarm was supposed to be halfway down the hall, near the science lab. Wily passed room 200 and 202, his heart beating so loudly he thought it would jump out of his chest. As they approached room 204, a lady in a pink suit exited.

Oh, no! It must be Ms. Feldor.

When she spotted Thor and Wily she stopped cold. "What is that dirty mutt doing here?"

Thor growled.

Wily clamped the dog's mouth shut. "Ah, he's part of a science experiment. I'm here to deliver him." He pointed down the hall. Wily's ears flushed.

"Does he have, er, that disease?" The lady took two steps back as if she were afraid Thor would contaminate her.

"Ah, maybe."

She waved her hand and ducked back into her office. "Go on, move along. Get him out of here." She sneezed twice as he hurried past her.

Wily hoped the guard didn't see Ms. Feldor and ask if she'd seen them. Ten more steps and he'd be at the fire alarm. He checked his watch. 9:15. *Mindia, where are you? You're supposed to pull it now.* The red box on the wall stared back at him. He'd have to pull it and hide in the closet. He spotted a door a few feet away and jiggled the handle. It opened. Phew. Inside were mops, a bucket, light bulbs, and cleaning supplies. There wasn't much room, but it would have to do.

"Wait in here," Wily said to Thor. "I'll hightail it in with you, so make room for me."

The dog whined.

Wily wrapped the leash around a mop handle and shut Thor in the closet. In two steps he reached for the alarm. And pulled. Instantly, a shrill sound rang out. He hurried back to the closet, opened it, and hid next to Thor, squeezing his eyes closed as if he could shut out the whole event, wishing he could wake up and this would all be behind him.

Someone shouted. "Where's that kid and the dog?" A two-way radio crackled.

Oh, boy. Wily stepped as far into the closet as he could go without landing in a bucket.

Doors in the hallway opened and slammed, footsteps sounded. Someone said, "Is there really a fire or is this a drill?"

"I don't know," another voice said. "Proceed out of the building. We have to assume it's real."

That sounded like the guard's voice. Right outside the door. If only Wily could see enough to notice if there was a lock on the inside. His fingers fumbled in the dark searching for the knob. He found it. Cold and hard. Careful not to make a sound, he placed his hand around the metal ball and felt for a center lock, one that he might twist shut or push closed. *Yes, he found it.* He twisted the raised notch until it clicked.

Seconds later someone rattled the door. "Kid, I know you're in there. Open up."

Wily didn't breathe.

The man pounded on the door. "If you don't open up I'm going to get a key, and you'll be sorry. You're already in deep doo-doo."

Wily squeezed his eyes shut.

Thor's breath dominated the dank, small closet.

Wily wanted to cover his nose with the crook of his arm, but he didn't dare move.

The running feet and excited voices outside the door dwindled. Maybe everyone had vacated the building. Now, if only the guard would leave, then Wily could carry on and get out of there.

One more bang on the door. "Okay, kid. I'm going to get a key. You're not going to get away with this. You had your chance."

Wily waited until he didn't hear the man anymore. He turned the lock and opened the door a crack.

"Aha." the guard said. He reached in and yanked Wily out by the neck, his face inches from Wily's. "Who are you?"

Thor leaped out, teeth barred. He growled at the guard, snapping at his heels, then jumped up onto the man's legs.

The guard fell backward, releasing Wily. "Aaargh." His bottom hit the ground first, then his head hit the wall.

Thor barked and stepped onto the man's chest, snapping at him.

The guard covered his face with his hands and grimaced.

Wily ran, continuing down the hall. The lab was close. Hopefully he'd find it empty. He had to believe that Thor could hold his own.

Wily turned a corner and found a door. He opened it slowly and peered inside. The lab. Right where it was supposed to be. Overhead florescent lights illuminated the room. Rows of tables, cluttered with glass vials, microscopes, and machines were before him. Not a man or woman was in the room. He bounced on his tiptoes feeling like he had to go to the bathroom. No time for that. He had to find the vial.

CHAPTER SEVENTEEN

Wily twirled in circles in the empty room, uncertain where to look first. The room smelled of rubbing alcohol and antiseptic spray—the kind his mom used to put on his cuts when he fell off his bike. He wished she were here now. She'd know what to do. But she wasn't. He needed to figure it out. Soon. The technicians wouldn't be gone for long.

A row of centrifuges sat on the table to the right. They were the machines that spun blood and urine to test for diseases and infections. That's not what he needed. What he needed was probably locked up. Yes. They wouldn't keep the test tubes out in the open.

At the back of the room was a glass-cased wall filled with rows of test tubes of liquid. He ran to peer in the cases. Thousands of tiny glass tubes were perched on the shelves. He tried to open every cabinet door. All were locked.

He searched for the keys in a nearby desk. There were only pens and pencils and scrap pieces of paper. He opened another desk drawer. Five bite-size Kit Kat bars stared at him. His mouth watered. He quickly reached in and scooped two of the bars from the drawer and shoved them into his pockets.

He hesitated.

That was stealing. He fished them out of his pockets, returned them to the drawer, and sighed. How could he think of candy at a time like this?

He needed to focus. Pick the locks. He dug in his pocket again, this time for his Swiss Army knife. He moved to the case, and flipped open the awl blade. Positioning the point inside the lock, he jiggled the knife.

Nothing happened. This lock was different than the one at home and on the ship. His heart raced. He tried again, this time jiggling more aggressively. On his third attempt, the lock engaged and the door to the case opened.

Yes. Vials clanked on the shelves. His heart did double-time. *Get the vial.*

But which one?

Each tube had a number. If only he knew what the numbers meant. Which one was the right one? He glanced at his watch. 9:35. He didn't have much time. Think. Where would someone put the number codes? Probably in a computer.

That would take forever to find.

He sat at a computer desk. The screen was open to a page filled with icons. He had no idea what to click. Sweat dribbled down his back.

He rose and went back to the wall cabinet, then noticed another cabinet with a solid front instead of glass. He inserted the awl blade into its lock and jiggled it. After what seemed like minutes, this cabinet door opened. Taped to the inside of the door was a typed list with numbers in the left column and corresponding words in the right column.

Trailing the list with his finger, Wily scrolled through the words until he found one labeled BONE MENDER/CANINE, number 62. He was about to turn away to collect the vial when he spotted CENTAURS, number 75.

A test tube labeled *centaurs*? What could that mean?

He collected the vials from their perspective shelves. Vial 62 contained a yellowish liquid with an orange rubber stopper sealing the top. He reached for that one, pushed several others out of the way, and collected number 75 too. That one had a green liquid, but the same orange rubber stopper.

Muffled voices sounded outside the door. Wily had to hide the vials. If he wasn't careful they'd break. Hurry. Paper towels hung in a spool at a table. He took two sheets and wrapped them around each vial and set them down. He couldn't put the wrapped vials in his pants pockets. They were too big.

A white lab coat hung on a hook to his left. He slipped it on and fumbled with the buttons. Then he shoved the wrapped vials into separate pockets. He hurried to the door and listened. Muffled sounds. No barking. No growling. There was only one way to find out where Thor had gone.

He inhaled, twisted the knob, and peeked out the slit. When he didn't see anyone, he opened the door wider. A man in a suit walked down the hall, his back to Wily and his head bent toward a cell phone. The man rounded the corner out of sight. No sign of Thor, Mindia, or the guard.

Wily continued out the lab door and smoothed down the collar of his coat that had spiked up around his ears. A chair was jammed in front of the closet where Thor and he had hidden. The door rattled.

Wily paused on the other side. "Thor?"

Muffled sounds came from inside. Something or someone kicked at the door.

Wily knelt in front of the door. "Thor?"

"Get me out of here." The guard. Oh, no!

Wily needed to hurry out before someone saw him. He continued on his way, his breathing still as rapid as his heart beat and the ticking of his watch, which read 9:55. He had five minutes to get to the ship. He could do it. Especially if nothing stopped him along the way. He lifted his shoulders and strolled down the hallway like he belonged there, increasing the pace of his steps, but not too drastically.

As he approached the end of the hallway, the elevator doors dinged open and streams of voices sounded. They must have let the employees back in the building. He kept his head down. If only he could find the stairs. They were probably at the other end of the hallway, the direction that Mindia had gone. The elevators would be too crowded. Yes, he'd keep walking to the other end of the hallway and take the stairs down. Certainly he could walk down ten floors. It wasn't like walking up.

A woman in a light blue dress turned the corner before him. He followed her, trying to blend in. Several voices sounded behind him. He didn't dare turn to see who they were. *Keep going. Don't stop.*

By the time he made it down the hallway and saw the red EXIT sign, sweat had dampened his hair. He flung open the heavy metal door leading downstairs and reached for the banister. He took two steps at a time, heaving air in and out. The stairs were deserted, but a lady's perfume lingered.

At floor number five he slowed, out of breath. He heard hushed voices. *Keep calm. Don't look like you're in a hurry. Keep going.* He jutted his chin forward and pretended he didn't see the man and woman in the shadows on the third floor. He purposely stomped his feet hoping they'd clear out. Before he got to the third floor, the couple ran out and the door closed with a bang.

Finally, Wily was on the first floor. He'd almost made it. He opened the door to see the jerk, Mr. Hanger, with his hands around Thor's neck.

Thor's eyes met Wily's, his expression begging Wily to do something.

"Hey, let my dog go." Wily said. "Someone, call the police. This man has my dog."

A lady, who was leaving the building looked back.

"Call 911!" Wily hollered to her.

Her forehead wrinkled in concern and she pulled a phone from her purse. "I'm dialing."

The man squeezed Thor's neck tighter. The dog's tongue drooped out of his mouth and he made a throaty sound. His legs went limp.

The lady screamed and raced toward the man, attacking him with her purse, beating him over the head repeatedly.

He let go of Thor, who fell to the floor.

Wily raced to his side. "Get up, boy. You can do it. Come home now."

Thor stood, shook from head to the tip of his tail, took a few wobbly steps toward the door, and stumbled.

Wily latched onto Thor's collar with one arm and half carried him, and half dragged him. When he pushed open the door to the city outside, a man walked in.

As the door closed, the man said, "Hey. You can't go decking women. Where are your manners?"

Wily kept moving along the sidewalk, not looking back, certain they'd be trailed. "Let's fly. We're late. Are you okay?"

A horn honked. Wily jumped and waited for the car to pass.

Thor, his tongue out and drooling, stopped next to him.

They turned the corner, passed the tall, windowed building, and stepped into the dark alley. Wily glanced at his watch. 10:01. The sun had risen higher in the sky, turning the air warmer and the stench from the dumpsters along the alley more rancid.

Police sirens rang in the distance.

A whirring sound revealed the steps to the craft were being

lowered. Wily smiled, never so happy to see a set of stairs in his life.

Thor paused, lifted his tail, scrunched and pooped right there.

Wily laughed. "That will hold them back for a while." He scurried up the steps, eager to get away from the foul smell. Breathless, he greeted Doc with a high-five.

"You made it." Doc said.

If only Wily's father could see what he'd done.

Devon sat at the controls, his curly wig still on his head. "Glad you made it back, kid. Where's Mindia?"

"She's not here?" Wily asked.

Thor bounded up the steps.

"No. When did you last see her?" Devon asked Wily.

"When we arrived on the floor she asked to use the ladies' room and we never saw her again. Did you see her after that, Thor?"

The dog shook his head.

"Did she rescue you from that guard?" Wily asked.

Thor shook his head again.

"Then where is she?" Devon asked. "She escaped. I can't believe she took off without letting us know." He slammed his fist into the control throttle. "She probably had it planned all along." He lifted the wig off his head and chucked it across the room. "We counted on her."

"That doesn't sound like her to just leave us. Maybe she had to take care of something else." Wily scratched Thor's ear. "Besides, she has a chip. The DH will find her."

"There are ways around that," Devon said.

Muffled voices sounded outside the craft. Doc, Devon, Wily, and Thor watched through the glass window. The craft was still invisible to the outsiders, and since they were inside, they were invisible now, too.

"They were here a second ago and now they're gone," a different security guard said. "They couldn't have disappeared." He took a few more steps, looked down, and swore. "Who took a dump right here in the middle of the alley?"

Thor seemed to smile when the guard lifted his soiled boot.

Devon steered the craft into flight mode, the invisible shield still preventing anyone from seeing them.

"So we didn't get the tube?" Doc asked Wily and Thor.

Wily reached into his pockets and handed him the wadded paper towels. "There are two. Inside here."

"Nice job." He messed up Wily's hair. "Why are there two?" He slowly opened the paper towels to reveal the tubes.

"One was labeled BONE MENDER/CANINE and the other was labeled CENTAUR," Wily said.

"Centaur?" Doc asked.

Devon joined them, his forehead creased.

Wily stood and crossed to Doc, observing the numbers. "Number 62 is the serum they're using on the dogs."

"What do you suppose is in the CENTAUR one?" Devon asked.

"I'm not sure, but I don't want to drink it. I like being a boy," Wily said.

Thor shuddered.

"I thought we could use it as leverage," Wily said.

"Leverage?" Devon asked.

"I'm not sure what's in it, but the contents might get us what we want from the DH."

Doc's jaw dropped. "You're brilliant, kid." He squeezed Wily's shoulder.

Wily smiled. His body felt lighter than it ever had. "Thanks." If only his father would say those words. Just once.

Devon took the canine serum. "Put the CENTAUR vial back in that drawer over there." He pointed to a wall cabinet behind Wily. "It'll be safe there."

Wily took the vial, rewrapped it in the paper and set it deep in the back of the drawer.

The craft felt empty without Mindia. He searched the ground below, hoping he'd catch a glimpse of her. "What will the DH do when he finds out she's gone?"

"He'll track her. When he finds her, well, you don't want to know," Devon said.

No one spoke. They should have been celebrating, but not without Mindia. The joy had vanished like their craft.

"What if she returns to that spot and we're not there?" Wily asked. "Isn't that possible?"

"She can use her two-way if she needs us, but she won't. She's not coming back," Devon said, his voice low and empty. "She's been waiting for the opportunity to ditch us for a long time. She's probably the leak that Thor mentioned when he got shot." He shook his head. "I can't believe she stabbed us all in the back."

"That doesn't sound like Mindia," Wily said.

Thor patted Wily's leg.

"I'll be landing in one block," Devon said. "Doc and I will deliver the disk and the vial to the authorities. Wily, you and Thor wait in the craft until we return." He opened a drawer, reached in, and threw Wily a Snicker's bar. "Help yourself while you're waiting."

"Sweet," Wily said, proud that he'd returned the Kit Kat bars. He preferred a Snicker's anyway. He tore open the wrapper and bit into the bar, celebrating the rich and caramel, nutty center.

Several minutes later, the craft expelled a slow hiss as Devon lowered the ship into the police department parking lot in between the back row of parked cop cars. A few people in the distance walked in and out of the front door. Wily recognized the building as he'd been to it before on a field trip when he was in the third grade. The trees out front bloomed with white flowers. They were the same trees he had in his backyard.

He was so close to his home he could walk there. What would happen to him if he simply walked off of the ship? He remembered the chip embedded in his gut, his insides probably red and raw. He'd have to get the medallion to stop the process. But how?

The ship jerked slightly when it touched the ground. "Don't think about leaving here," Devon said. "He'll destroy your family if you do."

"Okay." Wily's voice sounded small.

"Here's how you open and shut the door." Devon pointed to the button on the sidewall near the exit door. Watch for us. Let us in when you see us returning. Do you think you can do that?"

Wily didn't like his condescending tone. "Yes."

Devon pushed the button and the door hissed open. The two men deplaned, taking the stairs one at a time, glancing right then left, before proceeding to the front door of the police station.

Thor leaped onto the cushioned window seat and yawned.

Wily sat in Devon's chair and stared at the controls. He took another slow bite of his chocolate bar and wondered what it would be like to fly the craft.

The sun peeked through a cloud low in the sky, casting a glare through the windshield. Wily swiveled in his chair and stared out the other way, watching the people walk in and out of the building. A man and woman exited the police station, their arms locked together. They were about hundred feet away.

Wily bolted out of his chair and pressed his nose against the glass, squinting. "Mom? Dad?" It couldn't be them. Maybe it was someone who looked like them. He observed the woman's walk, his heart pounding in his chest. She had the same gait as his mother, a hurried step with her chin jutted forward. It was her. He needed to see them. The candy stuck in his throat. He tried to swallow, but he couldn't get it down fast enough.

Thor snored and his legs ran in place as he dreamed.

Wily ran to the door and pressed the open button. This was his chance. It was now or never. The fresh spring air fueled his energy. He was going to see his parents, at last.

CHAPTER EIGHTEEN

"Mom. Dad." Wily raced, the chocolate dribbling down his chin. "Wait."

The couple stopped.

"Wily?" His mother's mouth hung open. "Wily." She screamed and ran to him.

They met on the sidewalk and threw their arms around one another. She pulled away and placed her palm on his cheek. "Where have you been?" Tears streamed down her face. "We were so worried. But you're here. You're really here. You're okay. You're eating chocolate." She chuckled, the tears glistening on her cheeks. She pinned his face to her chest.

He pulled away, laughed, and wiped his chin with the back of his hand.

His father threw his arms around Wily. "Where have you been?"

Tears filled Wily's eyes. He couldn't remember the last time his father hugged him. A shadow covered his dad's face like he hadn't shaved. Red lines squiggled in the whites of his eyes.

"The police have been looking for you. *We've* been looking for you," his father said.

"It's complicated. They can't know you found me. I can't stay."

His father took a step toward him. "What do you mean? Where do you have to go?"

Wily shook his head. "Please, don't make me explain right now. I'll be home as soon as I can, and then maybe I can explain, but right now it's too dangerous."

His mother clutched Wily's arm. "Dangerous? How?" Her voice rose an octave. She reached for his hand and took a step toward the building. "Come. You can tell the police all about it, and then you're coming home with us, and that's all there is to it. It doesn't matter where you've been—only that you're coming home."

"No, Mom." Wily peeled his hand out of hers. "You could get hurt."

"Hurt? Now listen here, son," his father said. "The police can take care of this. All you have to do is come with us and tell them what's happened." He nodded toward the police station.

Oh, no. He should not have done this. Doc and Devon were going to be ticked off.

His mother threaded her arm through Wily's and guided him toward the precinct door again.

Wily dug his heels in. This had been a mistake. He never should have fled the shuttle to see them. Devon had said the DH would hurt his parents.

His father's brow creased. "Why are you resisting?"

A dog barked, the noise drawing closer. Thor was approaching, his teeth bared, looking ferocious. He snapped at Wily's parents.

Wily broke free from his mother's grasp. "Thor, stop. These are my parents."

But Thor bit the bottom of Wily's T-shirt and tugged him toward the shuttle.

Wily's father stepped toward Thor, his fist out, ready to pound the dog.

Wily blocked Thor. "Don't hit him, Dad. He's not the bad guy."

Thor growled, his teeth still gripping Wily's T-shirt.

"I promise. I'll find a way to return," Wily said, "but for now we have to save the dogs. My job isn't over yet."

"Your job is not to save the dogs, Wily," his mother said, crying.

"Yes, it is. We're almost done. There are a few things left to do."

"Who's we?" His father continued to step toward them as Thor held Wily's T-shirt in the fist of his jaws, yanking him backward.

"Wily?" A voice shot out from the front door of the precinct. Devon's. He and Doc hurried toward Wily.

Great. He was in trouble.

"I can't leave you alone for five minutes without you blowing the whole mission," Devon said.

"Mission?" Wily's dad asked Devon.

Doc smiled at Wily's parents. "Look, all this can be explained. Let's stay calm and move toward the parking lot. We'll explain everything there. The last thing we want is to draw attention. Your son's life is in danger."

Wily's father looked over his shoulder. "What is that supposed to mean? And how are we supposed to stay calm? I want to know what's going on." Wily's father said, facing Doc.

Devon grumbled under his breath.

"I understand," Doc said, his voice almost a whisper. "Follow us, and we'll explain." Doc waved them on toward the ship.

Panic rose in Wily's gut. Surely Doc wasn't planning on kidnapping his parents too. If Wily told them to run, they wouldn't. If he told them to run and they escaped—the DH might still do something awful. But bringing them aboard the shuttle meant that the DH would meet them. There wasn't a perfect scenario.

"Run." Wily said to his parents. "Run away as fast as you can." He gave them both a shove. He hated knocking his mom off balance, but it would be worse for her if he didn't.

Wily ran toward the shuttle. The others followed.

His mother screamed. "Wily." She and Wily's dad followed close behind him, undeterred.

"You're such an idiot," Devon said to Wily.

Wily's face heated. How could wanting to see his parents be such an evil thing?

When they reached the stairs that hung in midair, looking like they led to nowhere, Thor continued his trek up.

Devon elbowed for Wily to follow. "Go. We're going to have to take your parents with us now."

Wily's heart tumbled down to his toes. Now he was responsible for their danger, too.

"Wait a minute. What's going on?" Wily's dad said, standing a few yards behind Devon.

"Mom, Dad, run. Go!" Wily shouted from the top of the stairs.

Wily's mom extended her arm to her son. "Wily. No, we're not leaving you."

His father pushed Doc out of the way, climbed two steps, and reached for Wily's arm. His father tried to yank Wily down the stairs, but Devon pushed Wily's dad into the shuttle.

His dad scrambled onto the floor.

"Ben." Wily's mom shouted. "Where did he go?" She sounded hysterical.

They were certain to draw attention.

Doc steadied himself and reached for Mom's arm, leading her up the stairs and into the craft.

A police officer ran out the front door of the precinct and shouted across the parking lot. "Stop."

Doc glanced over his shoulder as he approached the top stair. He climbed in and pressed the door's close button.

The cop ran toward the invisible craft, but when the stairs disappeared, he froze. With his hand on his holster, he trekked closer.

Wily was sure if someone said boo, the officer would faint.

Devon ran to the controls, pressed a few buttons and the ship hissed, jerked, and rose. "Take a seat. Now." He commanded.

Wily's mom hurried to a chair, one hand over her mouth, the other hand gripping the seat. She looked out the glass walls, her eyes wide.

Wily's father crawled across the floor and took a seat next to his wife, his eyes roaming the craft inside and skating across the landscape outside.

A nut from the Snicker's bar was trapped between Wily's teeth, reminding him of how his parents were now trapped, too. All because of his stupidity.

CHAPTER NINETEEN

As they flew back to base, no one spoke. Wily sat on the bench near the window with Thor, keeping his eyes on his parents who sat with their mouths open, their faces as pale as snow.

What would happen now? He gulped.

Devon shot Wily a frown.

Wily looked away. Even though they'd nailed the creeps that were killing the dogs, they'd lost Mindia and gained his parents. They should have been celebrating the victory. They'd saved so many dogs from dying.

"Why can't you all go home now? Why do you keep serving him?" Wily asked.

His father's forehead creased. "Who are you talking about?"

"You don't get it," Devon said. "I tried that once." He paused. "He killed the one person left in my family—my father. Now, there is no one."

"The DH killed your dad? I'm sorry." Wily's head spun. It was difficult to believe the DH was capable of killing someone.

Wily's mother whimpered. "Who's the DH?"

"I can't believe he's that heartless," Wily said. He held up a hand to his mother. "Everything will be okay, Mom."

Devon rose from the control seat and pushed Wily. "He *is* that heartless and don't you forget it."

"Hey," Wily's father stepped in front of Devon. "Keep your hands off of him."

Doc shot out of his chair and stood between Devon and Wily's father. "Let's not get carried away."

Wily's dad and Devon returned to their seats.

Wily slinked into his chair. "I'm sorry." He lowered his voice and looked at Devon. "What exactly happened?"

Devon stared straight out the front window. "He killed my dad. That's all you need to know."

"How?" Wily pressed him.

"I don't know how, but he did."

"He doesn't have the power of spells, so how?" Wily asked.

"Spells? Powers?" his mother muttered. "Please tell me what's going on."

Devon shrugged at Wily, ignoring Wily's mom's plea. "Maybe he hired someone to do it. I'm sure he's behind his death. I just don't know how he did it. I hate him," Devon said.

If that were true, then the DH wouldn't hesitate to kill Wily's mom and dad too.

Devon shook his head. "Let me be clear. The DH does not care about your family."

Wily gulped. If only he could come up with a plan to make the DH change his mind, to show him that he didn't have to control his crew the way he did. But how? "Does anyone know how the spell was cast—the one that transformed all the centaurs into dogs hundreds of years ago?"

"What are you talking about," Wily's dad asked.

Wily held up a finger. "One minute, Dad."

"What does that have to do with anything?" Devon asked.

"If we know how Cressida cast the spell before, maybe she has the power to unleash the power now."

"That's what she's been trying to do. If she could, then why wouldn't she have done that already?" Doc asked.

"Maybe there's another reason," Wily said. But he had no clue what that reason could be.

The TV monitor above the control panel lit up and the DH's face appeared covered in bandages. "Were you successful?"

Orbita rested on his shoulder, her eyes bulging, her throat pulsing.

Devon nodded.

The DH looked out past Devon. "Who are those people sitting behind you?" He bellowed, his words echoing across the glass walls, shattering Wily's hope.

Wily's mom paled.

His father stood and moved behind Devon, facing the screen. "I don't know who you are, but if you're the one behind my son's abduction, I'll kick your—"

The DH laughed. "We'll see about that. Mindia—silence this man."

No one spoke.

"Mindia? Where's Mindia?" the DH asked.

"She never made it back to the ship," Doc said.

A crash sounded from the DH's room like he'd thrown his hoof into a table. "What? Turn around and get her. Bring her back here."

"We don't know where she is." Devon said.

Orbita blinked and then her eyes rolled up into her head. She went limp and tumbled down toward the floor.

"Huh?" the DH caught her midair. "Darling. What is it?"

Doc stood. Thor leaned in. Devon paused. Wily held his breath.

"Orbita?" the horse asked. He faced the monitor. "She's not breathing." He lifted the frog close to his face. "Breathe!"

Devon smirked.

The DH held Orbita in his hands and moved away from the screen. Wily could hear him but no longer saw him. The centaur whined and cried. "No, you can't leave me."

"What's happening, Wily?" his mother asked in a shaky voice.

"That man is a centaur and he's in love with his frog who used to be a princess centauride hundreds of years ago," Wily said.

His mother gave him a puzzled stare.

"Hundreds of years ago there was a spell cast and all the centaurs turned into dogs. The DH kidnaps kids to train them to work on his behalf. He needs all the dogs to turn back to centaurs. That's why he took me. To save the dogs."

"He's a kidnapper?" His mother placed her hand on her chest.

Wily's father sat on the bench next to Wily. "Look, son, there's a way out of this." He kept his voice low. "I'm going to help you."

"Thanks, Dad, but I can do this on my own. You don't know the DH like I do. He's not as bad as you think."

Devon hammered his fist on the dashboard and glared at Wily. "You imbecile. He *is* evil. When are you going to get that through your head?"

"There's good in him somewhere. There has to be. Don't you see the way he loves her?"

Devon crossed the room and came face-to-face with Wily, his nose inches away, his hands clenched in fists. "Don't you see the way he hates us?"

"No, I see the way he's afraid of us. He's afraid of being alone, and he doesn't know how to make friends." Wily's voice was soft, but he didn't move. He kept his feet planted where they were.

"Wily, Devon's right. This horse sounds evil. People who kidnap kids can't be good," Wily's dad said.

"You don't understand, Dad." Wily went back to the bench next to Thor, his head bent. Why couldn't his father support him? Just once.

Devon returned to the controls, shaking his head.

Thor patted Wily's hand.

Wily sighed. Why couldn't his dad understand that violence wasn't the way to win peace? Instead, his father probably thought Wily was being too weak, too compassionate.

Doc sat in the seat next to Devon clicking more controls as they glided toward the mother ship, hovering over it, and then descending into the opening.

The DH's bandaged face appeared on the screen again. "Wily, I need you here. Now. Orbita is gone." His eyes were wild looking. Tears dripped down his face.

Wily's mom gripped her seat and closed her eyes tight.

His father chewed his lip.

Wily sat quietly, contemplating his next move.

Doc glanced at him over his shoulder. "He's going to want you to bring her back to life."

"What?" His mother's eye's blinked open and she leaned toward Wily.

The shuttle jerked as it locked into the mother ship.

His mother stifled a short scream. His father reached for her hand.

Wily's mouth went dry. The taste of chocolate and the sweetness of the moment were long gone.

No one said a word. Each exchanged glances. It was the first time Wily had seen fear in his father's eyes.

Devon stared straight ahead, his hands on his legs.

Doc was the first to stand. "Let's get this over with." He reached for the button to open the door.

Thor bounded off the bench and placed his paw on Doc's arm.

"We need to have a plan before you open that door," Devon whispered.

"He's right," Wily said. "But for once I have one. Follow my lead." Wily pushed off of the bench and crossed the craft to the door.

"No, Wily. This isn't a job for you. It's too dangerous," his father said, crossing the room to block Wily's path.

"Please, Dad. Trust me. I know what I'm doing."

His mother whimpered. "Let him go, Ben."

CHAPTER TWENTY

His father stepped aside. Wily hit the button on the wall with authority. The door hissed open, revealing the DH, tears streaming down his face.

Wily's mother gasped and stared at the centaur. She held her hand over her mouth.

The horse paced in the hallway. Orbita was cradled in his hands, her crown no longer on her head.

Wily had never seen the horse so agitated.

"Orbita died." The DH turned to Wily. "You need to bring her back to life." He took Wily's arm and pulled him down the hall, not acknowledging anyone else.

Wily's parents followed with the others.

The horse threw open the door to the infirmary, the place where Thor had lain the previous morning, and placed Orbita on the gurney. Her tiny body filled only a small spot on the bed. "Where's your machine?" He licked his lips repeatedly.

"It's in the closet," Wily pointed and turned to Devon who'd entered the room with the others.

Devon paused.

"What?" the DH said.

Devon nodded toward Wily as if waiting for Wily to implement his plan.

"Look," Wily turned to the DH. "I will help under one condition."

"Condition?"

"You free the kids on this ship."

The DH kicked the closet door with his hoof, the sound cracking across the room and splintering the door. He kicked again, blasting a hole.

Wily's father held Wily's mom near the exit door.

Thor stood near Mr. and Mrs. Coldren with his tail drooped between his legs.

Wily crossed the room to Orbita and stroked her cold body. She smelled like a dead fish, like the frogs he'd worked on at home, the ones that had died along the creek in his backyard.

The DH paced, tears dripping down his face. "She usually eats twenty flies a day, but she didn't eat any today. She likes to bathe in the water and hop around from rock to rock, but she hasn't moved since you left this morning." Suddenly, the DH took a hold of Wily's neck. His nostrils flared. "Did you curse her?"

Wily's mother shrieked and his father demanded, "Let go of my son."

The DH loosened his grip and laughed. "Oh, is Daddy coming to the rescue?"

Wily coughed and rubbed his throbbing neck.

Doc patted Wily's father on the back. "Look, this isn't helping." He nodded to the horse. "Think about what you're doing. You need the boy."

The DH glanced at Orbita and stepped toward the gurney. "We had plans together. A future. A world to save."

No one spoke. No one offered condolences.

Wily inhaled. "I'm sorry for your loss. Now you know how the rest of us feel about losing our families."

The DH turned and slapped Wily, knocking him to the floor.

His mother screamed.

His father stepped forward, his fists clenched.

Devon restrained Wily's dad.

Wily put his palm to his cheek, feeling the heat rise like the other times.

Thor ran to Wily and licked his face.

Doc stooped to help Wily up.

"You don't understand," the centaur cried, glassy-eyed. "There are many of you."

"You don't understand," Wily said. "There is only one of me, one of Devon, one of Mindia. Even though there are many in our species there is still only one of us. Our feelings matter too. We don't want to lose our families either."

"Shut up," the DH said, lifting Orbita to his lips.

"I will help you, but you have to agree to my terms," Wily said.

Devon leaned forward. Doc released Wily's dad.

"You will bring her back?" the DH asked. He placed Orbita back on the gurney.

"Only if you give me and my friends freedom and remove the chips."

Devon smiled.

The DH paused and raked his fingers through his hair. Then he licked his lips as if he were nervous, as if he couldn't decide. He took a step toward Wily. "I order you to bring her back to life."

Wily didn't flinch. "You think that ordering people around to get them to do what you want them do will make you friends?"

The DH waved his hand. "I don't need friends."

"You will now that you no longer have Orbita. She was your only friend. And she's gone."

The others surrounded the DH and Orbita, who still lay on the gurney.

"I've waited years for her to be a centaur again," the DH said. "I'm sorry, my love. I'm so sorry. What have I done?"

"You didn't kill her, did you?" Wily asked.

"No, but I was the one who asked Cressida to cast the spell. It was me who turned my kind into dogs."

Devon snickered.

The DH glared at him.

Even though Wily had suspected that the DH had been behind the whole spell, it was sad to hear him admit the whole thing. "Can't you have Cressida undo the spell and turn the dogs back into your people again?"

He shook his head. "It won't work."

"Have you tried? Can't you cast spells too?" Wily asked.

The DH shook his head. "I can't. Don't you see? Something worse could happen."

"Like what?" Wily asked.

"I could … turn myself into … a frog." The horse lowered his voice.

Devon snickered louder and muttered under his breath. "It would serve you right."

The DH lunged at him and squeezed his neck. "What did you say, boy?" He shook Devon.

Mrs. Coldren screamed.

Thor placed himself between Mrs. Coldren and the DH.

The DH loosened his grip on Devon. "You think I was the one who killed your old man, but I wasn't. He killed himself. He was nothing but a drug addict who owed the wrong people money."

"You're lying," Devon said.

"I didn't want to tell you, but I'm sick of how you keep blaming me," the DH said. "Think about it. You know it's true. Was he ever there for you? For your mother?"

Doc took a step between the two. "Let it go."

The DH faced Orbita again. "Cressida has been working on

another way to undo the spell, but so far she's been unsuccessful."

The door opened and Wily's parents moved to the side, his mom still clinging to his father's arm.

Mindia entered ushering Cressida by the arm, only this Cressida was no longer a centaur, but a human. Mindia shoved her toward the center of the room. "Here you go."

"Mindia." Wily smiled.

Thor padded to Mindia and licked her hand.

"We thought you went home," Devon said.

"And leave you guys?" Mindia said. "No chance. I had to figure out who was the snitch, and I had a hunch, but I needed to check it out without anyone knowing. It appears that Cressida has had an ulterior motive. She's the one behind all the dogs dying. Look at her. She's been human by day—when she works in the lab, and centaur when she's here."

The DH snorted and crossed the room to face Cressida. "Look at you. Is this true? Have you betrayed me?"

Cressida stared at the wall, avoiding the DH's gaze.

"I trusted you. How could you do this?" He smashed his hoof into the closet again. "Why?"

Cressida frowned. "I can do so much more this way, more than I could ever do as a centaur. People don't look at me like I'm a freak. They respect me. You can be the same … if you drink the serum … if you become an immortal human like me. I've found a way." She moved excitedly toward the DH.

"And abandon my race? Never. Why would you think I'd agree to that? You were supposed to find a way to undo the spell, to turn the dogs into centaurs, not turn us into humans. Is this what you've been doing all these years?"

She shook her head. "There's no way to undo the spell. We have to wait until 2050, and I decided that it's much more appealing to turn into an immortal human like me. You can do the same." She leaned toward him, her hands on his shoulder. "Don't you see? Orbita will never love you—even if she returns as a centaur—which she can't. She's a frog forever, incapable of giving you the love you deserve. I'm here. I'll be here forever. I want you to love *me*, not that slimy toad." Her eyes shifted to the gurney where the frog lay on her back. Cressida gasped. "She's dead?"

"You killed her," the DH said.

"I did not." Cressida moved toward the gurney. "I saved you from a life of pain. And now," she turned to Wily and pointed at him, "he has the potion to make you a human. He stole it from the lab."

The DH turned to Wily. "Are you in on this too?"

"No, I had no idea about any of this." Wily stammered.

Mindia faced the horse. "Cressida needed no help working her corrupt wand. She's been the leader of the entire dog problem from the beginning. She was working with the thugs. She was leading them, working experiments to find a way to kill the dogs so the thugs could have their longevity potion and stop the spell at the same time. And she would have succeeded if it hadn't been for us, and especially you, Wily."

"What did I do?" Wily asked.

"You took my place when I vanished. You confiscated the potions. You were brave," Mindia said.

"Thank you, Mindia," Wily said.

"Where did you put the CENTAUR vial?" Cressida asked between clenched teeth, moving to face Wily.

Doc intervened. "Let the boy go. He's done nothing wrong."

"I worked years to make that potion." She looked at the DH. "Don't you see, if you drink that serum, you'll be a human, and if all the dogs die, none of them will turn into centaurs?" She waved her hand at Doc, Wily, Devon, and Mindia. "You'll all be free to go. There will be no revolution because there will be no dogs to return as centaur forms. It'll never happen. There will be no centaurs."

"You were killing people's pets," Wily stated.

The DH whinnied, the high-pitched noise chilling, silencing everyone in the room. "You were killing off the whole centaur race. We would have been extinct if these kids hadn't found the problem." He faced Wily. "If you save Orbita. I will let you return home with your parents."

"No!" Cressida exclaimed.

Wily shook his head. "I won't help unless you deactivate our chips and let us *all* go."

"I will only let you and your parents go." The horse stomped his hoof. "*After* you bring Orbita back to life."

"No. That isn't the deal. You must let everyone else go," Wily said.

The horse's face reddened. He gritted his teeth. "Okay, but *you* must stay then."

"No," his mother said.

"You need to think of yourself, son," his father said.

"These are my friends, Dad. If this is the only way to free them, then I will stay." Wily said.

Devon moved to Wily's side. "Thanks."

Cressida kicked the air toward Wily, but missed his shin. "Give me the CENTAUR serum."

Wily flinched.

"None of this other stuff matters," Cressida said. "The DH must comply, or he will be alone. There is no way to know if the centaurs will ever return."

"What?" the DH shouted. "You said in two hundred years the spell would be broken and all the dogs in the world would turn into centaurs. Did you lie?"

Cressida chuckled. "You're such a fool. Anything can happen between now and then. What if that day never comes? Do you want to take the risk?"

The DH shoved Cressida. After she regained her balance, he squeezed his hands around her shoulders and shook her. "Don't say that. It's my only hope. Why did I trust you?"

Cressida tried to claw him. Her face turned crimson.

Wily, Devon, and Doc pulled the horse off of Cressida.

Wily's parents watched, standing near the exit door, Thor at their side.

The DH clenched his fists. "It's no use. I have built my empire for nothing. I'm ruined." He ran his fingers across the cold frog. Then flung himself around and faced the others in the room. "If I let you go, I'll be alone. Forever."

"If you keep us here, you'll be alone. Forever. You can't force people to be your friends." Wily frowned.

"I don't need any friends," the horse said.

"Don't you?" Wily nodded to Orbita. "You do now."

"Please, bring her back to me, and I'll let you all go. I promise." The DH's voice lowered in defeat. He sighed.

Cressida laughed. "You believe him?" she asked Wily.

Mindia slipped her hand into Wily's and faced the DH. "Cressida has a point. Why doesn't Wily bring Orbita back and both of you can drink the serum and return to our world as one of us?"

"And forget about the centaur race?" He cocked his head.

Mindia nodded. "Yes. You would no longer be a freak. You'd be one of us, but so would Orbita."

"I agree," Wily said. "It would be the best for everyone." He went to the closet, gathered his black box off of the floor, and carried it to the gurney beside Orbita, where her stench grew stronger. It seemed ridiculous to help a frog, but if it meant freeing all of them, Wily would do what he could.

"Please, think about what you're doing," Cressida said to the DH. "Why do you want this slimy creature when you can have me? What has she ever done for you? You have an empire here." She waved her hand at the people in the room. "Don't give it all away. I found the way for you to do great things as someone other than a freak. Don't succumb to the stupidity of making her human, too."

Anxiety paced back and forth behind the DH's eyes. He shoved Cressida again.

She lost her balance and fell backward, smacking her head against the tiled floor. Crying out, she rolled onto her side and curled into a ball. "She's nothing but an amphibian piece of slime."

"Take her out of here."

"Where do you propose I put her?" Doc asked.

"Below. In the dungeon until … just take her away. I don't want to deal with her now," the DH said.

"I will expose you," Cressida said. "Your existence will no longer be a secret. People will laugh at you. They'll capture you and put you in a zoo, a museum. You'll be the freak you are in front of all the people."

"I will drink the serum," the DH said. "Wily will resurrect Orbita and then she and I will both drink this serum you claim to have made. We will live together as humans."

Cressida's cries grew louder. "No!" She crawled and wiggled toward the DH, kicking. She glared at Wily. "He'll never let you go free. And if he doesn't kill you, Orbita will. Mark my words. She's not capable of loving anyone. If she becomes human, earth will never be the same again."

"Take her to the dungeon." The DH waved his hand toward Doc and Devon.

Doc and Devon each took one of Cressida's arms. She went limp in resistance, so they dragged her out.

Her words hung in the air like a foul odor. She was right. Orbita wasn't capable of loving anyone. If Wily brought her back to life, it could change the world. But if he didn't, they would never go free. "Before I begin, you must deactivate the chips from the kids on this ship and set them free." Wily crossed his arms, dead set on not moving.

The DH's face reddened. "I will do no such thing." He crossed the room to Wily's mother and drew her in a headlock.

Wily's father fought to free his wife, but he was no match for the horse's strength.

The horse shoved Mr. Coldren across the room.

Mrs. Coldren shrieked.

Wily shouted, "Dad."

His father landed in a heap on the floor.

Thor crossed the room to Mr. Coldren.

Wily held up his hand. "Okay. Let my mother go. I will bring Orbita back to life."

"Where is the serum?" The horse still held Wily's mother in a headlock.

Wily paused.

The DH stomped his foot.

Wily nodded to Mindia. "It's in the top desk drawer in the shuttle. Way in the back. Wrapped in paper towel."

"Go get it," the DH said to Mindia.

Mindia turned to go.

"Hurry," Wily said.

Minutes felt like hours before Mindia returned. Wily had never seen his parents more beaten down or his mother more frightened.

Finally, Mindia entered the room with the serum. Breathless, she held up the vial.

"Put it next to Orbita," the DH said.

"Free Wily's mother first," Mindia said. "Or I'll smash this on the floor."

The DH released his whimpering mother who scurried across the room to her husband, her hands rubbing her blotchy neck. Mr. Coldren hugged her to his chest.

"Let them go," Mindia said, nodding to Wily's parents. "Or else." She made a motion to throw the vial.

The DH scoffed. "Get out of here," he said to Wily's parents. "Go."

"Not without our son," Wily's father said.

"Dad, please go. Take Mom," Wily said.

His father looked at his wife and then at his son as if contemplating what to do.

"No Wily. We're staying with you," his mother said.

"Very well then. Suit yourself," the horse said.

CHAPTER TWENTY-ONE

Cressida's cries echoed down the hallway as Devon and Doc dragged her to the basement.

Wily contemplated his choices. He could try to bring Orbita back to life. Or not. Cressida's words stuck in his mind. His actions to resurrect Orbita could have deadly consequences. He took a long breath.

Mindia stood to his right. "Don't listen to Cressida."

Thor nudged Wily with his nose.

Wily's father placed his hand on his son's shoulder. "You don't have to do this."

"Yes, he does," boomed the DH. He stabbed his elbow into Wily's father's side.

His dad lost his balance, the blow knocked the air out of him.

His mother screamed. "Ben."

"If you don't stand over there," the DH said, "and stay out of my way, I'll have you thrown in the dungeon too."

"Step aside, Dad. I'll be okay." Wily had never told his father to get out of his way. But he had to do this alone. He turned to the DH. "I'll try to bring her back, but I can't promise it will work."

"You better hope it does or you and your friends will die here," the DH said.

Wily gulped. His mom sobbed into her hands. He wanted to go to her and hold her, tell her that everything would be okay, but he didn't know what was going to happen. His machine had worked before. Certainly it would work again. But the frog was so tiny compared to Sport or Thor and even the rats.

With trembling fingers, he set the stiff frog on her back, plugged the machine into the wall, and rearranged the sticky electrode. This time he used only one thin-wired electrode like he'd used on the rats. He fastened one pad to the little frog's head. He hoped it wouldn't be too much electricity. He did mental math on how many volts it might take and adjusted the voltage meter. The last thing he wanted to do was fry the frog.

He watched Orbita's unmoving, bulging eyes, and held his breath. Then he glanced at Mindia.

She nodded for him to proceed.

The DH breathed over Wily's shoulder.

His parents had moved to the head of the gurney, their eyes glued to Wily, their mouths open.

Wily took a deep breath and flipped the switch.

Orbita's body jerked. Her legs fluttered. A twitch pulsed in her neck, bobbing in rhythm. Her eyes popped open and glowed, seeming to focus. She glanced at Wily then the DH. Then she rolled over and hopped onto her webbed feet.

"She's alive," the DH said.

Mindia gave Wily's arm a congratulatory squeeze.

Wily, swelling with pride, flipped the switch off and disconnected the sticky tab on her chest. His invention worked, and his parents had witnessed the miracle. He looked up them.

His mother's eyes filled with tears, but she smiled.

His father's eyes were filled with tears too. "Well done, son. Unbelievable. Now I see why this is way cooler than a baseball game." His father moved to Wily's side and threw his arm around him. "I'm sorry I doubted you."

Wily tingled inside. Finally, he was good at something his father respected. His dad saw Wily as he'd always been—an inventor.

The DH lifted Orbita into his hands and brought her to his lips.

Gross.

The door to the room burst open. "Cressida escaped," Devon said, breathlessly.

Everyone turned.

The DH slammed a hoof on the floor. "You imbeciles. How?"

Devon swallowed. "She tripped Doc and he fell, putting a gash in his head. When I bent to help him, she kicked me, but I escaped. She locked Doc in the cell and she's on the loose. I don't know what she will do."

The DH threw a fist into the air, bit his lip and ran a finger over Orbita. "We have a potion for you to drink that will turn you into an immortal human. Would you like to be transformed? It's not possible to make you a centaur, but this could work out better. What do you think?"

Orbita's eyes seemed to grow larger. She hopped out of the DH's hands and onto the gurney.

The horse lifted the vial off the gurney. "Bring me a little petri dish for her to drink out of." He nodded to Mindia.

Mindia searched shelves, cupboards and opened drawers. In the last one, she found a small plastic petri dish.

"Only give her a small dose at first," Devon suggested.

The DH swallowed, his Adam's apple bulging. "How can I trust Cressida? What if we turn into monsters?"

"She loves you," Mindia said. "She doesn't want to harm you."

The DH guffawed. "That's what she says, but I'm not sure."

Orbita hopped to the edge of the gurney, near Wily's dad, and rubbed against his hand. His father flinched and stepped away from the frog.

The man-horse examined the contents in the vial, twisted off the cap, and took a sniff. "It smells like honey." He poured a few laps in the petri dish and positioned Orbita in front of it.

No one said a word. The room stilled. Everyone gathered around the gurney. The only sound was the humming of the overhead florescent light.

"Go ahead. This is your chance," the horse said. "You will be an immortal human forever. We will be together as man and woman for once." His voice turned gentle, loving. He stroked Orbita's back, urging her toward the dish.

She moved to the liquid, bent and shot out her tongue. It curled toward the serum, slurped, and curled back into her mouth.

Nothing.

"Go again. Drink more," the DH said.

Thor watched, his head cocked.

Orbita's tongue curled toward the serum again and again, each time filling with the thick formula. When the bowl was empty she belched, then hiccupped. Then she grew fatter and larger. Her skin transformed from green to a flesh color. Her pink tutu ripped into shreds and fell to the side, exposing pink flesh.

Mindia gasped and reached for a long lab coat that hung on a hook in the corner of the room. She flung it over Orbita's growing, naked body as it began to transform in front of them.

The frog's back legs became long and lean human legs beneath the coat. Her two front legs shifted into arms that hung at her sides, ending with soft long-fingered hands. The final shift was her face. It went from a green toad-face to princess—soft ivory, petal-like skin. Long dark tendrils of hair curled down the sides of her face. Where once there were warts, now there was a set of high cheekbones and the greenest eyes Wily had ever seen.

Wily could see why the horse had fallen in love with her. She was beautiful.

The DH gasped. "It's you … my love. It's … really … you." His words came out disjointed, sort of like he was sobbing. "I've waited … so long … to see you." He wiped his damp eyes with the back of his hands.

Still sitting on the gurney, Orbita slipped her arms into the lab coat and examined her legs, turning them one way then the other, as if trying to figure out how they worked, seeing herself for the first time. She shifted her legs over the side and stood on wobbly legs—standing at least six feet tall. Then she tightened the coat around her to cover her bare flesh.

Mindia stepped forward to fasten the buttons.

Wily's parents took several steps back, their eyes wide, their foreheads creased.

"Does anyone have a mirror?" Orbita asked as she patted her face. Her voice sounded smooth, even, and melodic.

Wily's mother fainted. Her husband caught her and moved her limp body to a chair in the corner.

Thor barked.

Mindia moved to the desk where she'd found the plastic tray, reached in and pulled out a compact case with a mirror. "Here."

The DH stood by Orbita's side, tears in his eyes.

The new woman took the mirror from Mindia and opened the case. She smiled. "Oh … I *am* beautiful."

"Yes, you are. You always were," the DH said. He placed his hand on her arm. "I want to hold you. Please, let me hold you."

Orbita pushed him away. "Don't come any closer. You smell like hay."

The DH's expression changed into a frown. He shoulders fell at Orbita's reaction. "My dear, remember that it is because of me that you're finally free. Should I have kept you a frog?"

"You don't scare me," She waved her hand and moved toward

the door. "I've had to smell your horse-breath for the last time. Keep your distance." She turned to Devon. "Come with me. Show me the way. I want to see what Cressida is up to."

"Don't take her, Devon." The DH turned to Orbita. "I beg you to wait. Cressida will kill you."

She let out a shrill laugh that sent goose bumps down Wily's spine.

Orbita flicked her hair over her shoulder. "Let her try." With those words she took Devon's arm and wobbled out the door, her backside swaying like a movie star's.

CHAPTER TWENTY-TWO

Dark Horse hurried out the infirmary door after Orbita and watched her descend the stairs with Devon. "You're going to get yourself killed, my love. Please wait until I drink the serum, so I can go with you."

"I don't need your help or your love." Her laugh rang out again, bouncing off the tiled stairwell. "I can manage on my own." She held onto the banister.

Hearing Orbita's smooth voice speak in such an evil tone toward the horse made the hair on Wily's arms stand straight up.

The DH clopped back into the infirmary, ripped the bandages off his face and winced. He lifted the vial off the gurney and removed the stopper.

Wily glanced at Mindia who nodded, as if it was okay for the DH to swallow the serum.

Wily's mom wrapped her arm around Wily's waist.

The DH took the serum bottle, threw back his head, and drank three large gulps of the liquid. He grimaced, burped and waited. The air around him smelled of sweet honey.

The others in the room took a few steps back and waited.

The DH groaned, reached for his gut, and doubled over.

"What's happening?" Mrs. Coldren asked.

"I'm not sure," Wily said.

The DH's back legs buckled and he fell to the floor. His legs curled inside his body until they disappeared. His front legs lost their horse hair, turning to flesh. Feet and toes sprouted from where his hooves had been. His dark-haired mane vanished, and his body twisted into softer human features. On all fours, with his head hanging low, he arched up, pushing off the ground until he stood. His dark overalls hung loose on his body, and the pant legs only reached to his ankles. His chest was bare but hairy.

Wily had never seen a taller man. He was a giant, looming over all of them. Wily's dad was six foot, three inches, but the DH stood at least four inches taller than him.

"Wow," Wily said. "Amazing."

The others chimed in. "Unbelievable."

Thor growled.

The DH's eyes were the same dark ones, but his face appeared softer and gentler. His ears had lost their pointed look. If his face hadn't still been blistered from the fire, he might have looked like a rugged movie star. He held out his legs and turned them side-to-side, examining his new body. "Fantastic." He twirled on his tiptoes, lost his balance and set his hand on the wall. "It's awkward. Feet are different than hooves." He laughed nervously.

"You'll get used to it," Wily said, chuckling.

The DH reached for the compact mirror on the cabinet top and studied his reflection. "Maybe Orbita will think differently when she sees me now."

Wily doubted it. She seemed uninterested in him in any form. He had a feeling the only person she cared about was herself. He didn't trust the woman as a frog or a human. Cressida's warning still rang in his ears: *You'll be sorry if you resurrect her.*

"Let me lean on you," the DH said to Wily.

"Lean on me instead," Mr. Coldren said, offering his shoulder to the DH.

"Thanks, Dad." Wily said.

Together, they filed out of the infirmary—first Mindia and Thor, then the DH and Wily's dad, and lastly, Wily and his mother, her arm threaded through Wily's.

The DH stumbled, but Mr. Coldren helped him regain his balance.

As they traveled into the hallway, Wily's mother's eyes roamed—searching up, left, right, seeming to notice her surroundings for the first time, her eyes darting.

"It's a bizarre place, isn't it?" Wily said under his breath.

She nodded and squeezed his arm. "I thought I'd never see you again. I never dreamed you were in such a place. How did you find—?"

Mindia gave Wily a warning look.

Maybe it was better not to mention Mindia's gifts to his mother. "I'll tell you later," Wily said to him mom.

The DH hesitated at the stairs, grabbed the railing, and stopped. "Let's take the elevator."

After they made their way to the elevator down the hallway, Mindia pressed the button and the motor whirred, stopped, and dinged. When the door opened, they piled in. They only had to descend one level. Mindia pressed the "D" button.

Did D stand for down, dungeon, or death? Wily didn't like the sound of any of the options. His heart sunk to his toes as the elevator descended. His mother gripped his arm tighter.

The women's shouts rang out before the door opened. Cressida's shrill cries rang out above Orbita's harrowing laughs.

"Who's in charge now, you little beast?" Orbita said. "For years, I couldn't do what I wanted to do to you. Every chance you got you pinched my skin and flicked your fingers at me. Well now it's my turn."

Orbita had Cressida in a headlock. Both were lying in a dark cell on a cold floor. The damp air was charged with fear and danger. The cell door stood ajar.

Doc lay in the corner of the cell, his back propped against the wall, his head bloodied from a gash.

Devon and Thor hurried in and stooped at Doc's side. Devon examined the wound.

Wily and his parents waited outside the cell.

Mindia followed to Doc's side. "Should I get bandages?"

"No," Doc said, his breath raspy. "Just help me up. I'll be okay." He worked to stand.

Devon and Mindia helped him up and out of the cell.

The DH hovered over the women. "Stop right now."

"This is—," Cressida said, "the woman … you love … the evil toad who will never love you—." Her words were cut off by a blow to her head.

Devon, Doc, and Mindia exited the cell.

Wily tapped Mindia's arm and exchanged a glance. *Can you take hold of Orbita's thoughts, make her listen to you?* He didn't have to speak the words.

Mindia nodded at Wily and returned to the women who were fighting in the cell, pulling hair, slapping, and biting each other. She faced Orbita. "Look at me. I'll show you what to do." Mindia's eyes spiraled in their frenzied way.

Orbita stood and laughed. "You can't control me, little girl. Be gone." She waved her hand. "I won't look at you."

Mindia moved to get Orbita's attention, but when Orbita avoided her, Mindia left the cell.

Orbita paused and turned her eyes to the DH, as if seeing him for the first time. "Well now, look at you." She circled him, her eyes skating across his new body.

Cressida was still on the ground, rubbing her head and appearing dazed.

"Orbita, don't—," the DH said.

"—I'm going to hate getting rid of you now," Orbita said.

"What are you talking about? We are the same now. Don't you see? You can do anything you want. We can live together forever."

Orbita wrinkled her brow and turned up her nose. "I must admit you're better to look at this way, and you smell better, but there's only room for one ruler on this ship—and it's me." She shoved the DH against the wall. She was several inches shorter than the DH, but seemed much fiercer.

Wily gasped.

The DH lost his balance and shrunk back, his mouth open.

She pushed him again.

This time his head hit the metal bars of the cell and he fell into a heap.

"Don't let her hurt you," Wily said. "Fight back. You must."

Devon turned to Wily. "What are you doing? Let them kill each other."

"Don't you see?" Wily said. "He is going to let us go. She won't."

Devon paused. "He will never let us go." He lowered his voice. "The only way to get out of here is to go now." His voice was barely above a whisper and was directed to all of them.

The DH still lay on the floor, watching Orbita attack Cressida again. His hand rose to where the blood dripped from a gash on the back of his head. He appeared dazed.

Devon returned to the inside of the cell and crossed toward the DH. "Let me help you up."

The DH looked up at Devon, his head cocked like he wasn't sure what was happening.

Instead of giving the DH his hand, Devon gripped the medallion from around the DH's neck and yanked it. The medallion and chain fell into Devon's hand.

The DH shouted. "Hey."

Devon ran out of the cell, leaving Orbita, Cressida, and the DH inside the enclosure. He slammed the door shut and turned the lock.

"No." The DH scrambled to get up, but collapsed again.

Devon, Doc, Thor, Mindia, Wily, and his parents ran to the stairs.

Orbita and Cressida ceased fighting.

The cell doors rattled violently.

Orbita howled. "Let me out of here."

"Don't leave me here," the DH said, his voice trembling and pitiful.

Devon took the lead as they ascended the stairs. "Keep going until you get to the space shuttle. Do not look back. Go. Now."

CHAPTER TWENTY-THREE

The team made it to the first floor and paused.

"I'm taking you home," Devon said. "Right now. Head toward the shuttle."

They hurried down the hallway toward the craft.

Wily was elated that he'd finally get to go home, but he didn't feel right leaving this way.

Mindia slipped her hand into his. "It's the only way. Don't you see? He wouldn't let you go, and who knows how this is going to end?"

Wily paused and faced her. "You're right. He's never going to change, is he?" But he wanted to believe that anyone could change if he or she desired it.

They approached the entrance to the shuttle ship. Their loud breaths surrounded them.

Nora approached, running down the hall. "What's happening?"

Doc took her hand. "Come with us, and we'll explain everything."

"Where are you going?" she asked.

"I'm taking Wily, his parents, and Mindia home," Devon said.

Doc gave Nora a short version of what had happened.

Wily interrupted. "We can't leave the rest of the kids here."

"I'm coming back after we get you home. Now that I have this," he held up the medallion, "I can release everyone. All I have to do is turn the dial, and no one will be trackable. There's no way anyone can find you again."

Wily sighed. "That's all?"

Mrs. Coldren placed her hand on her heart. "Praise God."

Devon pressed the button to the shuttle and the door hissed open. "Let's get in."

Nora paused. "I'll stay here with the rest of the kids." She wrung her hands. I'll explain everything and reassure them that you're coming back for them."

Doc took her hands. "Thank you. We might not be back until late tonight."

"We'll be here," Nora said, her voice cracking.

Wily turned to Nora. "I'll never forget your meals."

"I'm sure you won't." Nora chuckled.

They hurried into the craft, waved good-bye to Nora, and shut the door.

Devon sat in the control seat. "Before we take off, let's deactivate your chip sensors."

Wily and the others gathered around Devon.

Devon dipped his hand into his pocket, took out the medallion, and turned to Doc. "How does it work?"

"Turn the notch all the way to the left, and it releases all chips within a ten-foot range."

Wily placed his hand on his abdomen.

"It won't hurt," Mindia said to him. "You won't feel a thing."

"How do you know?" Mr. Coldren asked, setting his large hand on Wily's shoulder.

Doc nodded. "It's no different than swallowing a piece of food. It will pass through you, and you'll never know it."

Mrs. Coldren sighed.

Devon held the medallion out. "Are you ready?"

Everyone nodded. All eyes were on the medallion. No one said a word.

Wily froze.

Devon moved the notch to the left. It clicked.

No one breathed. Seconds flew by.

Wily exchanged glances with the team before he finally took a breath.

"Woo hoo!" Devon shouted. "Let's get going." He high-fived everyone, then took a seat at the controls.

Everyone shouted.

Wily jumped up and down.

Thor barked.

Devon set course and flew the invisible glass shuttlecraft away from base.

The sun glowed in the distance, only an hour from disappearing into the night.

Wily sat on the bench next to Mindia, with his parents on the other side of him.

Devon insisted that he be the one to deliver Mindia and Wily's family to their homes. "I don't have anyone to go home to," he said. "My family is gone. It's only right that I take you home and return to the ship to help the others."

Doc sat in the co-pilot seat with Thor at his side.

Thor barked and placed his paw on Doc's arm.

Mindia laughed. "I guess Thor is going to stay with you, Doc."

Thor's head bobbed.

Doc patted Thor's head. "Of course. He's a part of the family."

Thor showed all his teeth. Drool spilled over his jaw.

Mindia, Wily, and his parents waved good-bye to the mother ship.

Wily scanned below for familiar stores and homes. He sat quietly, feeling queasy as the ship rocked. He was excited to go home, but sad because he'd miss his new friends.

"We'll keep in touch," Mindia said.

Wily smiled, but he knew it wouldn't be the same. "Take Mindia home first."

"No, Wily," she said. "If it wasn't for you none of us would be going home. You and your parents should go first."

"I'm not going home yet." He hugged his black box sitting next to him. "There's something I have to do first."

"What?" His mother and father asked in unison.

"You'll see," he said. "Besides, Mom taught me that girls always go first."

Mindia smiled and nodded to Mrs. Coldren. "Thanks."

Wily turned to Mindia. "By the way, how did you know that I would get the vials when you disappeared at Helms and Johnson? How did you trust that I would go through with your part of the plan when you didn't show up?"

She winked. "I knew all along you had the courage, but you needed to prove it to yourself."

"Thanks for believing in me." She knew him so well. Yes, she could read his mind, but she understood him, too. She understood his fears and his dreams and his weirdness, but she still was his friend.

"Yes, I am," she said and winked.

Wily blushed.

Devon looked over his shoulder at Mindia. "How did you know that it was Cressida behind the dead dogs dying?"

"When we arrived on the tenth floor," she said, "I caught a glimpse of someone who looked like her ducking into a room. But this woman was human. It was bizarre. I followed her. I found her at a conference table with Hanger and Jeffries, giving them a demonstration on how everything would work in the next phase. She didn't know I was listening in. I waited until the men left, and I approached her. I put her in a trance and she led me to her shuttle ship." Mindia raced to the window. "There's my house." She sighed. "So much has changed."

"What will your mom say when she sees you?" Wily asked.

Mindia shrugged. "Hopefully she won't have a heart attack. She probably thinks I'm dead."

Devon lowered the craft to the field behind Mindia's home. She hugged Devon and turned to Wily, smiling with tears in her eyes.

Awkward.

Wily knew she wouldn't hold back. She never had before.

She threw herself into his arms and kissed his cheek. "I'll see you again soon."

It felt strange to be good friends with a twenty-one-year-old girl and think of her as someone his age.

"I hope to see you again, too, Mr. and Mrs. Coldren."

"Thank you, Mindia," Wily's parents said in unison.

Devon pressed the buttons on the door and it hissed opened, letting in the fresh smell of cut grass and meat on a BBQ grill. Wily's stomach begged for food.

Devon let the stairs down.

Mindia skipped out and waved at her friends on the ship. She pointed to her mother who was stooped over in the garden, her back to the craft. Mindia's smile widened, bursting with excitement.

Devon closed the stairs and the door hissed shut.

They watched Mindia from inside the ship.

"Hi, Mom." Mindia stood frozen, staring at her mother's back.

Slowly, her mother turned and squinted. "Mindia?" She gasped, dropped the tiny digging tool in her hand, and ran to her. "Mindia. Is that you? You're really here?"

Within seconds, Mindia was in her mother's arms.

Her mother cried. She rocked Mindia in her arms. "I knew you would be back. I knew it. I've waited … for this … day." She pulled away from the embrace and took Mindia's face in her soiled palms. "You look the same. You … haven't changed. How … is … this possible?"

Mrs. Coldren, watching Mindia's reunion from the shuttle, wiped a tear from her eye and went to Wily's side. "I'm proud of you." She wrapped her arm around him.

Mr. Coldren wrapped his arm around Wily's other side. "I'm proud of you too."

Wily never thought he'd hear his father say those words.

Devon sighed and raised the ship. "There's nothing like a family reunion."

"I'm sorry you don't get one," Wily said.

Devon waved. "I'm over it now. At least I get to watch your reunions and share your happiness." He took the ship higher, gliding it back over the city. "Where am I taking you, Wily?"

"Back to the old Justin Mill Factory," Wily said.

Devon nodded.

"What's at that old place?" Mr. Coldren asked Wily.

"Dead dogs," Wily said.

Mrs. Coldren squealed. "That's where they were taking them?"

Wily nodded.

"Well, I'll be doggone," Mr. Coldren said under his breath.

When Devon reached the alley next to the factory, he brought the craft down to the ground and parked.

"This might take a little while," Wily said. "Will you bring my parents home and circle back to get me?" Wily lifted the black box from the seat next to him.

"No. We're going with you," Mr. Coldren said to Wily.

Mrs. Coldren set her hand on her husband's arm. "Let him go, Ben. Devon will bring him home."

Mr. Coldren protested, but Wily's mom put her finger over his lip.

Wily's dad shrugged. "I guess he can handle it, can't he?"

Wily nodded. For once, they were going to let him do what he wanted.

"I'll take you home next, Mr. and Mrs. Coldren." Devon pointed to Doc. "As long as it's okay with Doc."

"I don't have anywhere to go," Doc said. "As long as I'm with Nora, I happy."

Devon nodded to his computer. "Okay then. It's all set. I'll take your folks home, Wily, circle back here, and watch Star Wars on the computer until you return." He opened the door and lowered the steps for Wily.

His parents hugged him. "Be careful," Mrs. Coldren said.

"See you at home." Wily held the black box in one hand, the electrodes dangling at its side, stepped down, and looked both ways. Thankfully the alley was empty. He waved to the disappearing steps.

CHAPTER TWENTY-FOUR

Wily approached the Justin Mill Factory. The city streets were deserted. The sun had dropped behind the building and the air had cooled. He shivered.

When he reached the entrance to the factory, the door was locked, just as he expected. He chuckled. Last week if this had happened, he would have walked away, but not today. A locked door wouldn't stop him now from saving the dogs.

He set the box on the ground, slid his hand into his pocket, and pulled out his Swiss Army knife. It took him several attempts to jimmy the lock, but finally the door opened.

Once inside, he let his eyes adjust to the dark and found a light switch. He flicked it on and followed the hallway that led into the main factory. Several dead dogs lay on the conveyer belts, but he was sure they hadn't been forgotten—at least, not by their owners.

Holding his nose, he found a box of gloves at one of the workstations, plucked two out and put them on, trying to breath only from his mouth. He walked up and down the assembly line searching for Pookie. He saw German shepherds, Dalmatians, Irish setters, hound dogs, beagles, and rat terriers, but no white fluffy bichons. Nausea rose from the stench and the filthy flies buzzing in the room.

How could anyone leave these animals here like this?

One by one he hooked each dog to his box until they grew warm and full of life again. In half an hour he was drained from his work and surrounded by wagging tails and long pink tongues slurping his face. He found a bucket and filled it with water for them to drink. He thought he had looked everywhere for Pookie when he found a heap of dogs in a wheelbarrow near the entrance. He'd walked right past them without realizing it. He lifted each dog and placed them on the now empty conveyer belts. Near the bottom of the stack, he finally found Pookie, almost unrecognizable.

Wily lifted the little dog, then placed him on the conveyer belt. He thought of Mrs. Flannigan and how happy she would be to see her dog alive. He smiled as he pictured the reunion. He hooked the dog to the box and waited. It didn't take long for Pookie to get warm and glow. Wily watched as the pooch came to life. His eyes opened, his tongue turned pink, and his legs moved like he was running in a field.

"Hello, Pookie. It's nice to see you again." He hugged the pooch to his chest.

The dog whined and licked Wily's face. His tail wagged double-time.

Wily laughed and set him on the floor.

Pookie ran in circles. The other dogs chased him and welcomed him.

After Wily rescued the rest of the dogs, he peeled off his rubber gloves and threw them in the incinerator. Then he climbed the stairs into the office area and found a desk phone. He dialed 911.

"What's your emergency?" the operator asked.

"There's a warehouse full of dogs at the old Justin Mill Factory at 145 Center Street in Bluebird that need to go home. Come quick. They're hungry." He hung up and ran down the stairs. The dogs followed him like he was the leader of their pack. Before exiting through the front door, he lifted his black box in one arm and Pookie in the other.

He turned to the other dogs. "Someone will be here soon to feed you and bring you home again. It won't be long now."

A few dogs barked.

He closed the door, leaving them inside, and slipped out into the dark night. The sun had set. The clean fresh air welcomed him. When he made it to the spot where Devon had dropped him off, the stairs appeared out of thin air. Wily climbed into the craft with Pookie still tucked in one arm and his box in the other.

"Well done," Devon said.

"Any problems?" Doc asked with Thor at his side.

"None. There's a pack of dogs who are ready to go home—just like me." Wily sighed.

#

Devon lowered the ship to Mrs. Flannigan's green lawn.

The lamp in her front window was lit, and her outside lights illuminated her sidewalk.

Pookie ran to the window of the shuttle and barked.

"Are you sure you don't want to come home with me?" Wily asked Devon. "I hate being an only child."

Devon chortled. "No, thank you. But I'll come for a visit sometime."

"Promise?"

"Promise." Devon embraced Wily and patted his back.

Thor slapped Wily's face with wet kisses.

Wily hugged the large Dane.

Pookie circled Wily and growled at Thor who was unfazed by Pookie's aggression.

Wily lifted the small dog into his arms. "What will you do with DH, Cressida and Orbita?"

Doc spoke first. "Nora will put them to work in the kitchen."

"You're going to let them out?" Wily asked Doc.

"Only after they can prove that they are trustworthy, which will probably be never," Doc replied.

Devon shook his head. "We'll have our work cut out for us, especially since they're going to live longer than us, but we'll convert them to caring people, or they'll live a miserable life behind bars."

Wily shivered. He had a feeling that Devon wouldn't hesitate to *take care of them* if he had to. He drew Thor into a tight squeeze and then Doc. "I'll never forget you guys."

Doc snickered. "I bet you won't."

Pookie squirmed in Wily's arms and jumped down, running in circles and barking.

Devon lowered the stairs.

Pookie padded down the stairs and out of the shuttle.

Wily ran after the dog, still carrying his box.

The dog ran up Mrs. Flannigan's porch steps and to the front door. He scratched obsessively, adding to the other marks still visible there.

Wily hurried after the dog, climbed the steps, and rang the bell.

Footsteps sounded and Pookie barked and panted.

When the door opened, the dog practically flew into Mrs. Flannigan's arms. Wily thought she'd faint she looked so shocked from the assault. A small cry came from the woman's mouth, but her look of surprise quickly changed to one of joy. Tears fell. She pressed the dog to her chest. "Oh, my sweet Pookie. My boy, my sweet boy. How can this be?" She met Wily's eyes with puzzlement. "How? What? Where did you go? Everyone was looking for you."

"I've been trying to find a cure for your dog, Mrs. Flannigan. I'm sorry it took me so long, but I have to go home now." He waved and stepped off her porch. "See you later."

She stood there with her mouth open and Pookie licking her face.

"Thank you, Wily. You're a good boy." She talked baby talk to Pookie and set her nose next to his.

Wily crossed the street in the dark. His house hadn't changed. Yet, he had. It felt like he'd been gone a month. He saw everything differently. The grass was greener, the hyacinths fuller and more fragrant. He walked through the front door. "I'm home."

His mother, with a spatula in her hand and wearing her favorite black and white apron, came from the kitchen. "Are you hungry?"

"You bet I am." He went to her, dropped his box, and crossed the room to the pan on the stove. "What's for dinner?"

A bark sounded from somewhere in the house. Toenails skirted across the tiled floor. Sport came running. At first the dog hesitated like he wasn't sure who Wily was, then he tackled Wily, knocking him over and smacking his face with wet kisses.

Wily laughed and flailed his arms, squinting and blocking the slurps.

The back door into the kitchen opened and his father entered wearing a baseball cap, a football jersey, and shorts. "Welcome home, Wily."

"Thanks, Dad. It's great to be here."

Wily scrambled to rise from the floor.

His father gave Wily a hand and embraced him. He wrapped his large hand around Wily's head, hugging it to his chest like a football. "We … missed … you." His words were disjointed with emotion. "It's good to have you home safely. I thought we'd lost you. Forever. And I thought it was my fault." His voice cracked. He took a deep breath. "That was quite an ordeal, wasn't it?"

Wily nodded.

"You aren't kidding," his mom said. "Spaceships, centaurs, magic spells, and serums. No one would believe us, would they?"

Wily laughed.

His father laughed harder.

Soon, the three of them laughed uncontrollably, bent over, and held their guts.

Wily had never been so happy or felt so loved.

The television on the kitchen counter flashed with a news bulletin.

"We interrupt your regularly scheduled program …"

They gathered in front of the screen to watch.

"An anonymous 911 call led police to the Justin Mill Factory in Bluebird minutes ago where ninety-eight dogs were found alive and waiting for their owners. The dogs are healthy and hungry. They are being held at the factory until the owners can be reached. If you believe your dog is among this pack," the video panned over the dogs for several minutes, "please contact the Bluebird Animal Rescue to claim your pet."

Wily's dad turned to Wily. "Did you do that?"

Wily smiled and shrugged.

"You did, didn't you?" His father whooped.

Sport ran in circles.

"In other news," the newscaster said, "the FBI arrested Mortimer Lassiter, the chief executive officer at Helms & Johnson Pharmaceutical Company, and Robert Hanger and Stephen Jeffries, scientists at the same company. A fourth suspect remains at large. Employees at the company said she was a tall dark-haired, green-eyed woman named Cressida, but there are no records of an employee matching that description. If you have evidence of her whereabouts, please contact the police authority in your city.

"Another anonymous tip led investigators to discover the deception that resulted in this canine pandemic.

"Top managers at Helms & Johnson were working to perfect a new drug to prolong life in humans. The ingredient needed to create this drug could only be found in canines that had ingested Energy Pet treats. These treats, manufactured by Helms & Johnson, carry a deadly canine virus. When the animals ingest the treats, the virus kills them. Once in their systems, the viral cells bind with the dog's spinal fluid and create the solution needed to prolong human life. This ingredient was being extracted from the spinal fluid of deceased dogs.

"If you have purchased these treats, please do not give them to your dogs. Bring them to your local animal shelter for disposal. The National Humane Society is working with authorities around the clock to stop this pandemic.

"The FDA is investigating how this product made it to the shelves and passed regulation guidelines."

The screen switched back to a commercial.

Wily's mother whistled, pulled up a chair, and fell into it. "What has this world come to?"

Mr. Coldren turned the television off and shook his head. "And to think that our boy was responsible for nailing these crooks." He ran his hands through his hair and beamed at Wily.

"I told you the scientists didn't know what they were looking for." Wily moved to the stovetop to stir the ingredients. "Can we eat now?"

CHAPTER TWENTY-FIVE

The next school day.

Mrs. Flannigan held Pookie on the leash in her front lawn and waved at Wily.

He waved back as he climbed the stairs of the yellow school bus.

"Hello, Mrs. Harp. How are you today?" he asked the driver as he boarded.

Mrs. Harp smiled at him. "You look different, Wily." She cocked her head. "Did you part your hair on the other side or something? You look … older … more confident."

Wily reached up and smoothed his hair. "Thanks."

Kids on the bus whispered as Wily entered. All eyes were on him. He passed Matt and Tyler on the way to his seat.

The boys watched him go past, but didn't taunt him.

He took his seat across the aisle from Katey Prichard as usual.

Katey smiled so wide that her dimples showed. "Hi, Wily."

He waved.

The bus shifted into gear and went a few blocks before it stopped again. The doors hissed opened and someone climbed up the steps. Wily looked up.

Mindia.

He bolted out of his seat with his mouth open.

She wore a pale blue shirt with ruffles along the bottom. The color matched the color of her eyes. Her blonde hair fell in soft curls around her shoulders. He'd never seen her with her hair down. She looked younger than he remembered.

Tyler whistled. "You can sit here." He shoved Matt out of the seat.

Mindia ignored him. Her eyes skated across the others on the bus until she met Wily's gaze. She waved. "Hi, Wily." She practically skipped down the aisle toward him.

"Hi," Wily said.

"Can I sit with you?" she asked.

"Of course." He fell back into his seat and scooted over. "What are you doing here?"

"I'm going to your school now," she said.

A flash of light appeared in the sky out of the corner of Wily's eye. He turned to look.

Kids on the bus turned to look, too. It had come from the north, the direction of Costco, but now it was gone.

Mindia giggled. "I wonder what's happening up there."

Wily wondered the same.

THE END.

A NOTE TO THE READER

I hope that you enjoyed reading *Wily and the Canine Pandemic*. There is no greater honor for a writer than to know that readers enjoyed her work. If you liked this book, please tell your friends and ask your mom or dad to post a reader review online at Amazon, Barnes and Noble, or wherever you purchase books. Reviews and word-of-mouth recommendations help support authors.

I'd love to hear from you, too. Send me a note and tell me what you think should happen next. Do you think there should be a book two? If so, whose book should it be? Mindia's? Wily's? Devon's? Or the Dark Horse's?

Here's my email address: Michelle@MichelleWeidenbenner.com.

I can't wait to hear from you!

ABOUT THE AUTHOR

Michelle Weidenbenner spends most of her time between Leesburg, Indiana and Citrus Hills, Florida. When she's not writing she's playing pickle ball, walking her dogs, or helping people uncover their stories. She calls herself the Uncover Agent. She's a writing and business coach who loves helping people hone their gifts and tell their stories, so they can make the world a better place. She prays that her legacy as the *Uncover Agent* will live on long after she's gone.

If you're a writer who wants to learn how to outline your book and write fast, download this free FAST DRAFT today.

If you're curious as to what it costs to self-publish a book, feel free to download Michelle's free PDF on self-publishing costs.

Michelle is a certified John Maxwell trainer, speaker and coach. If you'd like to schedule her for a speaking event, or hire her as your writing or business coach, contact her at:

Michelle@MichelleWeidenbenner.com

Michelle's Other Work

Cache a Predator, A Geocaching Mystery (An adult thriller)
Scattered Links
Fractured, Not Broken, a Memoir
The Éclair Series
    Éclair Goes to Stella's
    Éclair Meets a Gypsy
    Éclair Goes Geocaching

If you have a child who is an early reader, download this FREE e-book as my GIFT. Learn the story of how the Gypsy Vanner breed came to the United States.

Éclair Meets a Gypsy –FREE BOOK, visit
http://www.michelleweidenbenner.com/Gift/